Praise for The Country Club Murders

CLOUDS IN MY COFFEE (#3)

"A sparkling comedy of errors [illegible] mystery. I loved it!"

– [illegible] M. Boyer,
USA Today Be[illegible] Book Club

"Readers who enjoy the no[illegible] Susan Isaacs will love this series that blends a strong mystery with the demands of living in an exclusive society."

– *Kings River Life Magazine*

"From the first page to the last, Julie's mysteries grab the reader and don't let up."

– Sally Berneathy,
USA Today Bestselling Author of *The Ex Who Saw a Ghost*

"This book is fun! F-U-N Fun!...A delightful pleasure to read. I didn't want to put it down...Highly recommend."

– *Mysteries, etc.*

GUARANTEED TO BLEED (#2)

"Set in Kansas City, Missouri, in 1974, this cozy mystery effectively recreates the era through the details of down-to-earth Ellison's everyday life."

– *Booklist*

"Mulhern's lively, witty sequel to *The Deep End* finds Kansas City, Mo., socialite Ellison Russell reluctantly attending a high school football game...Cozy fans will eagerly await Ellison's further adventures."

– *Publishers Weekly*

"There's no way a lover of suspense could turn this book down because it's that much fun."

– *Suspense Magazine*

"Cleverly written with sharp wit and all the twists and turns of the best '70s primetime drama, Mulhern nails the fierce fraught mother-daughter relationship, fearlessly tackles what hides behind the Country Club façade, and serves up justice in bombshell fashion. A truly satisfying slightly twisted cozy."

– Gretchen Archer,
USA Today Bestselling Author of *Double Knot*

THE DEEP END (#1)

"Part mystery, part women's fiction, part poetry, Mulhern's debut, *The Deep End*, will draw you in with the first sentence and entrance you until the last. An engaging whodunit that kept me guessing until the end!"

– Tracy Weber,
Author of the Downward Dog Mysteries

"An enjoyable, frequently amusing mystery with a mixture of off-beat characters that create twists and turns to keep Ellison—and the reader—off-guard while trying to solve the murder and keep herself out of jail. The plot is well-structured and the characters drawn with a deft hand. Setting the story in the mid-1970s is an inspired touch...A fine start to this mystery series, one that is highly recommended."

– *Mysterious Reviews*

"What a fun read! Murder in the days before cell phones, the internet, DNA and AFIS."

– *Books for Avid Readers*

SEND IN THE CLOWNS

The Country Club Murders
by Julie Mulhern

THE DEEP END (#1)

GUARANTEED TO BLEED (#2)

CLOUDS IN MY COFFEE (#3)

SEND IN THE CLOWNS (#4)

SEND IN THE CLOWNS

THE
COUNTRY CLUB
MURDERS

HENERY PRESS

SEND IN THE CLOWNS
The Country Club Murders
Part of the Henery Press Mystery Collection

First Edition | October 2016

Henery Press
www.henerypress.com

Cover art by Stephanie Chontos

Trade Paperback ISBN-13: 978-1-63511-081-4
Digital epub ISBN-13: 978-1-63511-082-1
Kindle ISBN-13: 978-1-63511-083-8
Hardcover ISBN-13: 978-1-63511-084-5

Printed in the United States of America

For my father, who's always believed

ACKNOWLEDGMENTS

My thanks, as always, to Madonna Bock and Sally Berneathy, who suffer through first drafts, to Dash, Gersh, and Sunshine for being who they are, to my family who'd like me to take up cooking, and to my editors, Rachel, Kendel and Erin, who make me so much better.

ONE

October, 1974
Kansas City, Missouri

I've tripped over a body. I've run over a body. I've even swum into a body. I never imagined one would fall on me.

Then again, wandering around a place called The Gates of Hell, what did I expect?

How I came to be at The Gates of Hell is a story in itself. The short version is that my daughter, Grace, missed her curfew. It was a school night and she'd sworn on a stack of Emily Posts that she'd be home by ten. When I called her friends' homes, I learned that each thought she'd gotten a ride home with someone else. She'd been left behind. At a haunted house. In a neighborhood best described as sketchy. "Omigosh, Mrs. Russell I don't know how this happened," spoken in a breathless, apologetic voice didn't help. Not when Kim said it. Not when Peggy said it.

I threw on some clothes, drove to the West Bottoms, and explained to the man at the ticket counter that my daughter was missing.

He wore an eye-patch and a wrinkled shirt. He was unsympathetic. If I wanted to look for my daughter, I needed to buy a ticket.

I bought a ticket.

Just inside the door the world turned dark as pitch. I paused, let my eyes adjust to the dimness, then took a tentative step.

Ahead of me a group of girls shrieked that high-pitched squeal unique to teenagers and heroines in horror movies.

I shuffled forward, my fingers brushing against a wall that felt as if it had been constructed with particleboard. The wall ended and I touched something—someone—warm but somehow scaly.

Turns out almost middle-aged women can achieve that high-pitched squeal as well.

Before I'd entered the haunted house, I'd thought of Rodin's Gates of Hell. Tortured souls damned for all eternity. Something dark and twisted and artistic. Inspired by Dante. Rendered in bronze by the greatest sculptor of all time.

The thing I touched never crossed Rodin's mind. It never occurred to Dante. It was the stuff of nightmares—or horror movies. A red-faced demon with long teeth and horns, and—oddly enough—a frock coat.

Demons don't scare me. I've faced down monsters. Heck, I was married to one. "Excuse me." I yanked my hand away from his.

I walked on. Vampires and werewolves and a man with a running chainsaw—surely that couldn't be safe? Strobe lights. A maze. Squeals. Teenagers huddled together so tightly they moved at a snail's pace. The Gates of Hell had all of this. It didn't have Grace.

I tapped a girl on the shoulder.

She shrieked and whirled around, her hands clasped over her heart.

"Have you seen a single girl? My daughter is missing."

Her eyes grew large as if she thought I was part of the haunted house. A worried mother looking for a daughter who'd entered the Gates of Hell and failed to return. To me that was far scarier than the zombie bearing down on us.

The girl didn't agree. She screamed and ran.

Perfect.

I moved on. Searching in each room. Discovering hidey holes for the characters who terrorized kids eager to be scared.

I paused in a room that felt as big as a shoebox and called, "Grace."

Nothing.

Well, nothing if you don't count a man wearing an executioner's hood and bearing an axe. "My daughter is missing," I told him. "Have you seen a teenage girl by herself?"

He grunted and hefted the axe onto his muscle-bound shoulder.

Dammit.

The next room looked like a circus gone bad. Ripped red and white striped fabric half covered the walls and drooped from the ceiling. A popcorn machine with a head inside the glass sat in a corner. A demented calliope song was just audible over the screams of the girls in the room in front of me. And there were clowns.

Two of them.

I hate clowns. That's not strong enough. I abhor clowns. Clowns chill my blood. Clowns turn my normally reliable knees to the consistency of the tomato aspic the chef at the club serves at ladies' lunches in the summertime. I. Despise. Clowns. And those are the friendly ones at the circus who wear big shoes and cram into tiny cars.

Don't ask why. Some fears are just visceral. Snakes. Spiders. Clowns. Pick your poison.

These clowns weren't of the friendly variety. They had pointed teeth. They wore wicked expressions. And, despite the cheery ruffs at their necks, they were the stuff of nightmares. One of the clowns staggered toward me. Yes, he had a red nose. Yes, he had fuzzy hair. But he also had a grin evil enough to send my knees past tomato aspic straight to tomato bisque.

"Go away," I squeaked.

He raised a knife that appeared to be dripping blood.

I backed up until my shoulders pressed against the popcorn machine. The one with the head inside.

He advanced. "Missel ruthel."

"What? Go away." I held up my hands and splayed my fingers. "I'm here to find my daughter. I don't want to be scared."

"Missel ruthel."

A second, scarier clown stood in the doorway watching us.

Not only was the knife dripping blood, the clown was too. His polka dot suit looked as if half the fabric had been dipped in crimson.

"Go. Away."

The clown let the knife fall to the floor. "Mrs. Russell." His voice was twisted, as if forming words required enormous effort. Then he said it again, "Mrs. Russell."

The world shrank to a fanged clown with frizzy blue hair saying my name. Stars danced in my eyes. The calliope music echoed in my ears.

He stumbled forward, fell into me, and slid slowly down the front of my stiff body, tugging my new trench coat on his way to the floor. "Mrs. Russell, help me."

Was this some twisted trick? A Halloween prank? If so, it wasn't funny.

The other clown, the one in the doorway, tilted his head to the side. He too was covered in white face paint. He too wore a bulbous red nose. He too had frizzy hair. But his eyes, painted black, looked like an abyss.

When you look into an abyss, the abyss also looks into you. Or so said Nietzsche. I wasn't risking it. I returned my attention to the clown at my feet. The one who knew my name. The one who'd asked for my help. The one who wasn't moving.

I brushed off my sweater where the clown had touched me and found the Shetland wool wet. I brought my fingers to my nose and sniffed. The coppery scent of real blood filled my nostrils.

The clown in the doorway grinned.

A shudder ran through me and I dropped to my knees. "What happened?" I demanded.

The first clown grabbed my hand. He squeezed for an instant then his hold loosened.

I searched for a pulse with clumsy hands. Found nothing.

The clown in the doorway stepped into the room. He too had a knife. He looked as if he was ready to use it. On me? My blood roared in my ears, louder than a lion in the center ring. My heart plummeted like a trapeze artist who had missed the swinging bar.

I lunged toward the only weapon available to me—the knife the clown on the floor had dropped—my fingers stretched and strained, but the blade remained just out of my reach. The motionless clown lay in my way.

The other clown, the one with the dead eyes, shook his head and smiled bigger—as if my attempt to secure a weapon amused him.

My lungs refused to inflate fully. I panted for breath.

The remaining clown stepped closer.

A group of girls spilled into the room. They saw the clown with the knife and shrieked loud enough to cause hearing loss.

I abandoned the clown on the floor, lurched to my feet, and positively hurled myself toward the group of girls. With an evil, knife-wielding clown in the room, they didn't even notice me.

Nor did they notice when I worked myself into the center of their tight little knot.

I held my breath as we snail's-paced our way to the next room. This one filled with hairy spiders.

I glanced over my shoulder. The clown watched me, the shudder-inducing grin fading from his face but the full-on evil remaining in his eyes.

I was leaving the other clown, the motionless one, alone with him.

Here's the thing about terror...it's more immediate than guilt. With terror sending adrenaline coursing through my veins, I didn't care about leaving the polka dot clown behind.

I'd send help. Although, I suspected the man with the red nose was beyond help. I hadn't found a pulse.

It had been days since I found a body.

Glorious days.

My stomach tightened with dread. I was going to have to call Detective Anarchy Jones, the homicide detective who'd investigated my husband's mistress's murder...and my husband's murder...and...I tried not to think about the number of bodies I'd found. And now I was going to add a clown to that number.

Oh. Dear. Lord.

Maybe it was all part of the experience. Maybe the two clowns had been trying to scare me. I *was* in a haunted house.

Except...I knew the clown was dead. I'd found enough dead people to know dead.

I'd locate security. Tell them about the clown on the floor. I'd find Grace. Then I'd take her home, ground her until she went to college, and pretend the dying clown hadn't gasped my name. I'd pretend I hadn't witnessed a murder. I'd settle down to a night filled with bad dreams and the lingering vision of the second clown's blackened eye sockets.

I spotted a man in a guard's uniform, crossed my fingers that he wasn't a zombie, and left the safety-in-numbers group of teenage girls.

"Excuse me." I tapped him on the shoulder and claimed his attention. "Someone has been murdered."

He didn't react—much. He just tilted his head and leaned forward a bit, as if he meant to sniff my breath for alcohol. "Where's the body?"

"Several rooms back. The circus room."

The tilt of his head became more pronounced. "You do know the characters are trying to scare you?"

"Yes," I snapped. "I also know dead when I see it."

"Fine." The tightness near his eyes suggested that my *imaginary* dead clown was a huge inconvenience. "Let's go look."

"Shouldn't we call the police?"

"Let's have that look first." His voice was soothing, his demeanor unruffled. He'd even managed to relax the skin near his eyes. If he ever left his security guard gig, he could make a mint as a shrink.

"Also, my daughter is missing."

"Do you want to look for her or the body?" His voice was still calm, but I sensed a chink in his Zen armor. It was bad enough he had to spend his nights listening to screaming kids, now he had to deal with a crazy woman.

I swallowed my worry over Grace—an enormous lump of worry that lodged in my throat. She was a smart, a capable girl, she'd be fine. "The body." At least I knew where that was.

The guard and I backtracked, working against a flow of young people.

Finally, we reached the circus room.

Empty.

No dead clown. No clown with dead eyes.

I pointed to the floor. "He was right there!"

"Of course he was." The guard used his shrink voice on me.

I stepped farther into the room. My eyes scanned the shredded curtains for lurking clowns and found none.

"No body, ma'am. Lots of people going through here get scared and imagine things."

"I didn't imagine anything. He was right there." Again I pointed.

"Well, he's not now." The guard turned on his heel.

"Wait! I don't imagine things. I don't."

"What you saw was probably part of the act. The goal is to frighten you."

Goal achieved. "Clowns are scary enough without knives and blood. Besides, if they wanted to scare me, why knife each other? Shouldn't they threaten me?" Dead eyes had—sort of—but that wasn't information I felt compelled to share.

I crossed the dark room to the popcorn machine, bent and touched the floor. It was sticky with drying blood. "There's blood on the floor."

"Props, ma'am."

"And on my sweater? My jacket?"

A frown disturbed his too-calm demeanor. "The actors aren't supposed to touch you."

"Well, one of the clowns collapsed on me."

The guard crossed his arms and pursed his lips.

Had I convinced him?

"What was he wearing? We'll have to write him up."

"He won't care. He's *dead*."

"Then where's the body?

"Maybe the other clown hid it."

"Why?"

"I don't know." Why anyone would don a clown suit, much less commit a murder and hide the body, was a mystery to me.

It was the police's job to figure that out—well, at least the murder part. "I feel faint." I didn't, but now, because I'd lied, my nose itched. "I think I'd better sit down."

Now the guard looked concerned. His brow actually furrowed.

"Is there someplace where I might rest?"

He held out his arm as if I might not be able to walk without his support. "This way."

I took his arm. I even leaned on it. There was no need to let him know I didn't feel faint, didn't need a chair, I needed a telephone. And once I got that phone...the security guard might not believe me, but Anarchy would.

The guard led me to an office near the exit. A board with *condemned* painted across it covered the door. The guard pulled it open.

We walked into a modern office. Two desks. File cabinets. Phones. Coffee mugs filled with pens. Actual light that seemed extra bright after the darkness of the haunted house.

One of the desks was occupied. A woman wearing a turtleneck, a delectable tweed jacket and pearl earrings looked up from a ledger. "Yes?"

"This lady's daughter is missing and she says one of our clowns has been murdered. She doesn't feel well." What he didn't say—*here's another lunatic*—was louder than his actual words.

The woman peered over the top of her readers. Her brows drew together. "We only have one clown."

They had two. Well, now they had one. One of them was dead and his body was missing. The other one killed him. Not that the security guard believed me. Arguing would get me nowhere. I fluttered my hands near my throat. "May I sit?"

The woman nodded toward a chair. "Of course. People get scared and imagine things. Is there someone we can call for you?"

I sat and reached toward the phone. "May I?"

She pushed the phone across the desk.

"Thank you." I inserted my finger in the rotary dial and turned. I'm not sure what it says about me that I have a homicide detective's home number memorized...

He answered on the third ring. "Hello."

"Anarchy, this is Ellison calling."

Seconds ticked away. "Don't tell me you found a body."

"Um..."

"Unbelievable." A few more uncomfortable seconds ticked by. He sighed, a so-much-for-Johnny-Carson-haul-yourself-out-of-the-easy-chair sigh. "Where are you?"

"The Gates of Hell."

"Very funny."

"No. That's where I am. It's a haunted house in the West Bottoms."

"I'll be there in ten. Do not disturb the crime scene."

Even as we spoke, teenagers were tromping through his crime scene. And then there was the matter of the missing body..."About that—"

"Yes?"

I chickened out. "Never mind. I'll tell you when you get here."

I hung up the phone.

"Someone's coming? You'll feel better when you get home and put your feet up."

"She says the clown touched her," said the guard.

The woman's forehead furrowed. "We don't allow the actors to touch our guests. That's against the rules." She took off her glasses and rubbed her eyes. "Are you sure?"

I looked down at my navy blue sweater. It was too dark to show the clown's blood. So was my coat, a Gucci leather trench (I'd watched the thermometer for weeks waiting to wear it until the weather turned cool) that did no better revealing the clown's bloody handprints. Too bad I wasn't wearing the khaki Burberry I'd bought in London, then maybe she'd believe me. "I don't think you can blame the clown. He was dying at the time."

She shook her head. "We don't script dead clowns." She jotted a note on a legal pad. "Although it's not a bad idea."

"I found it terrifying."

The security guard snorted.

The woman shifted her gaze to him. "You can return to your post."

He nodded and slipped out of the office

"It will probably take a while for your ride to get here. Would you like coffee?"

"Please."

"Cream and sugar?"

"Cream."

A Mr. Coffee sat on a small table in the corner. I love Mr. Coffee. He and my father are the two men in my life who've never let me down.

"I go through a lot of coffee. October is nothing but late nights." She stood, revealing a suede skirt and to-die-for boots, poured me a cup, and brought it to me.

"Thank you. Have you worked here long?"

"I own the place."

I blinked back my surprise.

"I'm Priscilla Owens."

"Ellison Russell." I extended my hand.

We shook and she settled back into her chair. "Your daughter is missing?"

"She is." I bit my lower lip. "May I use your phone again?"

"Of course."

She was very nice. I liked her. She wouldn't be so nice when the police closed her down to investigate a murder.

I dialed home.

Grace answered on the second ring. "Mom? Where are you?"

Thank God. The tightness in my chest loosened. "The Gates of Hell. How did you get home?"

"I called a cab. I didn't want to wake you."

Translation—she'd hoped I'd sleep through her blowing her curfew and she'd be able to sneak in without my noticing.

"We'll talk about it when I get home." Now that I knew she was safe, the urge to kill her tightened my fingers around the receiver.

"I'm sorry, Mom."

"Cancel your plans for the weekend, Grace."

"But—"

"No buts."

"Mom, you can't ground me. It's the weekend before Halloween. There are a ton of parties."

"Too bad."

"It's not fair." The universal lament of teenagers.

"Life's not fair." The universal answer of worn-thin mothers.

Grace hung up the phone. Well, she slammed down the phone. I hung up the phone, settling the receiver gently into the cradle. "Thank you for letting me make that call."

"My pleasure. It sounds as if she made it home."

"She did."

"I bet the clown mystery is just as easily solved."

It was a good bet—for me. I didn't take it. Instead, I took a sip of coffee and glanced at my watch. Anarchy would arrive soon and then a real circus would begin.

TWO

Tap, tap, tap.

"Come in," called Priscilla.

A ghoul with skin the color of peat stuck his terrifying head in the office. Not just his head, his neck and shoulders appeared too. It wasn't as if he was a real ghoul who could detach his pate. "There'th a cop here who theth he'th looking for Ellithon Ruthell."

If I had three-inch fangs, I'd probably lisp too.

Priscilla's eyebrows scrunched together. "A cop?"

Anarchy Jones pushed past the ghoul and entered the office.

Priscilla whipped off her readers and replaced her furrowed brow with the stunned expression most women wear when they first encounter Anarchy. He's that good looking. Lean face. Coffee brown eyes. An air of danger. Kansas City's version of James Bond (if James Bond let his hair grow a tad too long and wore plaid pants).

It was impossible to tell if he even noticed her. His gaze caught mine and held. Then he strode across the floor and crouched next to my chair. "Are you all right?"

"Fine."

"What are you doing down here?"

I explained the snafu with Grace's friends.

"Have you found her?" He covered my hand with his and some of his warmth seeped into my skin.

"She took a cab home."

"I'm glad she's safe." He glanced around the office. "Where's the body?" His voice lost its soft edges. With a simple shift in tone, he sounded like a cop.

Priscilla stirred in her chair. "There's no body. Mrs. Russell got scared and imagined she saw a murder."

Anarchy looked at me, a question in his eyes.

I answered with a tiny nod.

"If Mrs. Russell says there's a body, there's a body. Where is it?"

"Missing," I admitted.

"Missing?" He stood and looked down at me. A frown pulled at the edge of his lips.

"Missing." Then I told him about the two clowns and how one of them knew my name.

He glanced at Priscilla. "Do you have access to personnel files?"

It must get annoying having people assume you're a secretary when you're the owner. I didn't blame Priscilla for the tightening near her eyes.

"Priscilla Owens, this is Detective Jones. An—Detective Jones, this is Priscilla Owens. She owns the place."

"Detective?" Priscilla paled to the exact shade of one of the ghosts wandering her haunted house.

"Nice to meet you." Anarchy extended his hand, waited until she reached across the desk and slid her fingers into his grasp, then executed a quick, no-nonsense shake. "Who plays the clowns?"

"One clown," she corrected, her voice as sharp as the knife that had killed the one clown.

"Who was he?"

Priscilla stared at the door, not moving, apparently lost in thought. Her pallor did not improve. Seconds ticked by. Long seconds. Finally she stood, smoothed her skirt over her hips, crossed to the file cabinet, and withdrew a slim folder.

She opened it, squinted, and touched the top of her head as if looking for her glasses.

"They're on your desk," I said.

"Thank you." Priscilla snatched her glasses off the ledger, settled them on her nose, and ran her finger down a list. The actor playing the clown's name was—" her body stiffened and her pale skin took on a near translucent hue "—Brooks Harney."

I gasped.

"You know him?" demanded Anarchy.

"A bit. I know his parents. Grace and his sister, Camille, are friends."

"Country club people?"

He made belonging to a country club sound like a disease akin to leprosy.

"Yes," I admitted.

"So what was he doing working here?"

My friends' grown children tend to enter medical or law school. That or they launch promising careers at banks or brokerage firms or in commercial real estate. Some work for their father's companies. A handful tour Europe for a year before coming home and settling into their lives. Brooks had done none of those things. "I didn't know he was in town. He went off the rails a couple of years ago."

"He was an exemplary employee." Priscilla closed the file and slapped her hand against the top of the cabinet. "Is an exemplary employee. This is ridiculous. Brooks isn't dead."

Brooks was dead.

"I'd like to see the circus room," said Anarchy.

"Fine," Priscilla huffed. She jammed the file back into the drawer and slammed the drawer shut. "This way."

We walked back to the circus room which was now entirely empty of clowns.

"I told you." Priscilla crossed her arms over her chest. "Imagination run wild."

Anarchy reached into his jacket and withdrew a slender flashlight.

"Where were you, Ellison?"

"I backed into that thing." I pointed at the popcorn machine with the decapitated head grinning at us from its nest of popped kernels.

Anarchy shone the flashlight on the floor. The shaft of light revealed a pool of liquid.

He crouched, touched the edge and brought his fingers to his nose. “It’s blood.”

I bit my lips, keeping the words *I told you so* locked behind my teeth.

Poor Priscilla looked ill. Very ill. She leaned against the wall.

“I’ll need to call this in.” Anarchy stood. “How many people have been through here tonight?”

“Thousands.” Priscilla’s tone was flat.

“The crime scene techs won’t like that. We’ll need to interview your employees.”

Priscilla answered with the smallest of nods.

“You’ll have to close.”

She nodded. “It’s almost closing time anyway.”

“I don’t when know you’ll re-open.

She tapped her wrist and her watch glowed red. “Tomorrow night. We re-open tomorrow night.”

“Ma’am—”

“Listen here, Detective Jones. We make thirty percent of our gross the week of Halloween. If you close me down, you put me out of business.”

“I’m sorry, ma’am.” Anarchy really did look sorry. He lowered his chin and his brow puckered.

“You don’t even know if Brooks is dead.” She cast a glance worthy of the evil clown my way.

Poor woman. She was in denial. I offered an apologetic shake of my head. “No pulse.”

“If ever there was a woman to recognize a dead body, it’s Mrs. Russell.”

That wasn’t exactly a compliment.

“There is no body,” Priscilla insisted. “Dead bodies don’t just disappear. I bet he got up and went for help.”

Anarchy shined his light on the pool of blood on the floor—the lake of blood. "I doubt that. I'll call the station house, see about getting Mrs. Russell home, and then talk to your employees." His hand closed on my elbow. "Where's your car?"

"The lot."

He led me toward the executioner's room. "I'll see you again in a few minutes, Mrs. Owens."

"Thank you for the coffee," I said. "And for allowing me to use your phone."

She didn't say *you're welcome.* I didn't blame her. Until I'd shown up in her office she had a viable business. Now she had a warehouse filled with scary props, no customers, and a large payroll (minus one clown).

The executioner was apparently off grinding his axe, or practicing his menacing grunt, or getting a drink—whatever it was that actors at a haunted house did after the doors closed.

Anarchy's steps slowed. "Tell me about Harney."

"What do you want to know?"

"How did he end up here?"

I glanced at a wall where fake heads hung on pikes. Anarchy posed a good question.

"Drugs." We passed through a torture chamber complete with a rack.

"A user?"

"His parents spent a fortune on rehab. It didn't work. Then they tried tough love." I could only imagine what tough love from Genevieve Harney felt like.

"That didn't work either?"

We emerged onto the sidewalk and I drew a deep breath of air not tainted by grease paint or fear into my lungs. "Brooks disappeared."

The story at the bridge table was that Brooks stole Genevieve's grandmother's pearls and hocked them. When the Harneys discovered the theft, they gave him a choice—another try at rehab or jail. Brooks selected a third option and left home.

"Do you know where he went?"

"No idea." When Brooks sank below the surface of the drug culture, his mother rededicated herself to worthy causes and his father worked still more hours. Who knew how Brooks' brother Robbie—away at college—took the news. Brooks' sister spent days crying in Grace's bedroom.

The rest of us—those who weren't particular friends with Genevieve and Robert—never mentioned him. At least not to his parents. On occasion his name came up over a rubber of bridge.

Genevieve and Robert never brought up their oldest son in conversation. Instead, they talked about Robbie—recently graduated from Yale and taking a year to work with his father before entering Harvard Law.

As for Camille's soaking tears, Genevieve solved that problem with boarding school.

"How long has Brooks been away?"

I stopped and thought. "A year, maybe two."

We walked toward my TR6 which sat lonely and vulnerable in the parking lot surrounded by hulking buildings with dark windows. Grit crunched beneath our shoes and a brisk October wind blew leaves and bits of paper along the cracked pavement. The same wind carried the muddy scent of the river that flowed cold only three blocks away. Anarchy tucked my arm in his. "We'll need you to come to the station tomorrow. Noon?"

"May I come later?"

"Why? According to you, there's been a murder."

"My father asked me to play golf with him. We tee off at noon."

"There's been a murder. Can't you play earlier?"

"No."

"Why not?"

"Women aren't allowed on the course until noon."

He considered that for a moment.

I'd considered it ever since Henry died. I was the member. I paid the club bill. I wasn't allowed on the course in the morning.

"Cancel," said Anarchy.

I shook my head. "I can't. Daddy wouldn't ask me to play golf unless he has something important to discuss. I can be at the station by four thirty."

The arm that held mine stiffened, bringing my elbow against Anarchy's torso. For an instant I imagined I could feel his heart beating.

"I could come earlier," I offered.

"It will take at least twelve hours to process the crime scene."

"So, four thirty?"

"Fine." He loosened his hold on my arm. "Where are your keys?"

I dug them out of my purse and handed them over. Our fingers touched. Lingered.

The troubling electricity that always seemed to arc between us sparked wildly.

It raised the hair on my arms. It sent shivers down my spine. It parted my lips in anticipation.

Anarchy's face looked harder than the business end of a five-iron. He unlocked the car door and returned my keys to me. "I'll see you tomorrow afternoon. Drive safely."

Maybe he didn't feel the electricity. "Anarchy." I reached for his arm.

He stepped out of my reach. A hurried step. One that said he didn't want me touching him.

Anarchy felt the spark. Hell, he probably smelled the burned ions in the air. I know I did. But Anarchy had decided to ignore or avoid this *thing* between us. I wish I could. Ignoring it would make life much easier.

My stomach, my spleen, maybe my heart—definitely my heart—contracted, squeezed by the sting of rejection. Rejected because I was keeping my word and showing up for golf with my father? The sting lingered like the last guests at a party, the one that refuses to leave despite broad hints about early mornings and busy days.

Dammit.

It wasn't as if Anarchy and I had a future.

After being married to Henry Russell, trusting a man again was a bit like one of those free-fall exercises where you fell backward and hoped someone was there to catch you before your head conked against the floor. It took enormous courage. Even when the man waiting with his arms out and ready was Anarchy Jones. Especially when the man waiting with his arms out and ready was Anarchy Jones. And now those arms were gone. I breathed fetid air deep into my lungs and held it.

"Ellison—"

I held up my hand for silence and exhaled. Then I lowered myself into the car and started the ignition. "Good night." He was right. He was. There was no sense in torturing ourselves when I'd declared I wasn't ready. I pulled the door closed and drove away, leaving him alone in that bleak parking lot.

I met Daddy at the club.

He waited for me in the parking lot, unloaded my clubs and insisted on carrying them to the golf cart. Then he drove us to the first tee.

He didn't say much.

I didn't expect him to. He doesn't usually say much until the dogleg on the fifth hole.

We parked at the men's tee box and Daddy pressed a tee into the turf, placed his ball, and withdrew a driver from his bag.

He bent, stared at his golf ball, tilted his head and glanced at the fairway, adjusted his grip, and swung.

The ball sliced into a stand of blue spruce.

"What's wrong?" I asked.

"What makes you think something's wrong?"

"You never slice."

He picked up his broken tee and walked toward me and the cart. "You need to talk to your sister."

"About what?"

"Giving away a kidney isn't like giving away last year's handbag."

My sister was donating a healthy kidney to my cousin David whose kidneys had been damaged by childhood diabetes. It was the only completely altruistic thing she'd ever done and she was positively basking in the glow of giving.

I walked down to the ladies' tee, set my ball, and swung.

The ball sailed down the fairway.

Daddy grunted his approval. "Nice ball. Your mother won't see reason."

I kept my lips firmly sealed and we climbed into the cart.

We didn't drive far. "Do you want some help finding your ball?"

"She absolutely ignores the dangers." Daddy shook his head, apparently bewildered by the rare occurrence of Mother disagreeing with him outright. "It's a major operation and your sister may need that kidney someday."

Marjorie doing something so out of character—so nice—had sent ripples through our family. Now that one of Mother's daughters was giving a kidney to Aunt Sis's son, the two were behaving like sisters should. Marjorie and I were actually getting along. Marjorie's husband Greg doted on her endlessly. Things were better than ever—one might say they were going swimmingly (if one wanted to tempt fate)—and Daddy wanted me to churn up the smooth waters?

We walked across the fairway in search of Daddy's ball. "That useless husband of hers won't tell her what to do."

So Daddy had already had this conversation with Greg and he'd refused to intervene? No surprise. He was so happy to have Marjorie back (my sister left him briefly for pastures that looked greener) that he was unlikely to say anything.

I spotted the ball nestled among some pine needles and pointed. "There it is. You should talk to her."

"I have. She won't listen."

"And you think she'll listen to me?"

"She might."

The only problem with Daddy's plan was that I agreed with Marjorie's decision. I was the worst person to try and talk her out of it. If David and I were a match, I'd have gladly become a donor.

"All I ever wanted for you girls was to have happy, secure lives." My father considered his sight lines then hit his ball onto the fairway. "Nice husbands." He slid his club back into the bag. "Men you could depend upon."

"Marjorie has that."

"Greg isn't looking out for her best interests."

I disagreed.

Daddy was still away. He took his third shot and the ball rushed toward the green. He scowled as if he'd hooked left. "What's wrong with a comfortable, stable life?"

"Nothing." My own comfortable, stable life had gone to hell when my dreams became more important to me than my husband's. Given that Henry had been murdered, it hardly seemed appropriate to say I was happier without him. I was. "But Marjorie's a grown woman, she can make these decisions."

"She's making a mistake."

I pursed my lips and approached my ball. "Maybe. But it's her choice—her life. And if it's a mistake, it'll be her mistake."

"What about her family? How is she going to take care of her family? This is major surgery."

"She'll have plenty of help."

"Her husband and her children should be more important to her than David."

"David is family too."

Daddy snorted.

I swung my club and sent my ball to the green.

"Nice shot." Daddy's tan cheeks looked sunken, and pouches had appeared under his eyes. He wore his worry on his face.

I slipped my club back in the bag. "She's not a child. She made this decision. We ought to respect it."

He shook his head.

"You and your sister will always be my little girls. You'll understand someday."

I wouldn't. I wanted Grace to grow up into a strong, independent woman.

"A parent always worries," he added. "The worry never goes away."

That I could agree with. We drove to the putting green in silence.

I climbed out of the cart and rubbed a kink in my neck. Golf was supposed to be a stress reliever, not a stress inducer. "Your ball is away."

Daddy lined up a twenty-foot putt and sank his ball.

"Nice." My own shot was closer to ten feet with a slight slope to the right. Not exactly a gimme but not terribly difficult either.

"I'll make a deal with you," said Daddy. "You make this putt, I'll drop the subject. You miss it and you talk to your sister."

I could talk to Marjorie until my face turned a deep shade of indigo and not change a thing. Her mind was made up. Daddy was behaving as if we were still fractious teenagers.

"Tell her I'll release her trust fund early. She can have it now." Marjorie and I both got full access to our trust funds when we turned forty.

"She doesn't need the money."

"No one turns down that kind of money."

"She gets it in six months anyway." Our trusts were set up to distribute when we hit certain ages. The distribution from the trust might take some of the sting out of forty.

"Well, then...tell her she can have the lake house."

"Daddy, she and the kids summer in Harbor Point. She doesn't need a lake house."

"Ellie..." Daddy turned my name into a sigh of frustration. "Would you please just talk to her?"

"If I miss the putt."

I missed.

THREE

I drove home rehearsing possible conversations with Marjorie in my head. I wasn't very convincing in any of them. But that was probably because giving David a kidney was the right thing to do.

My next-door neighbor, Margaret Hamilton, stood at the corner of our street, her eyes scanning the intersection.

Her cat, Lucifer, must have escaped again.

I waved.

She scowled.

I didn't stop. Just because she'd left her broom and peaked hat at home didn't mean she wasn't a witch.

I parked in the circle drive and glanced at my watch. I had less than ten minutes to clean up if I wanted to make it to the police station on time.

Aggie opened the front door before I inserted my key. "You're home."

Aggie is my housekeeper. She is a gem. Not even gems open the door before someone knocks.

"What's wrong?" I asked.

"Detective Jones called." Her brow was as puckered as one of the smocked dresses I made Grace wear when she was little.

I stepped inside. "And?"

"He has to reschedule." She shook her head. Her earrings, long, dangly ones made of silver palettes and purple beads, shimmied in the late afternoon light. They were mesmerizing.

"Did he say why?"

Aggie pursed her lips, raised one brow, and tilted her head to the side until the bottom of her earring brushed the violet cloth of her kaftan. Her expression was a cross between annoyance that Anarchy hadn't provided her with a reason and why-are-you-even-talking-to-Anarchy-Jones-when-you-could-be-with-Hunter-Tafft. My friends and family have fallen into two camps. Those who think I should make a commitment to Anarchy Jones and those who think Hunter Tafft and I are a perfect match. Hunter is suave. Hunter is charming. Hunter and I know all the same people. Mother and Aggie, whose late husband used to work for Hunter, are very much in the Hunter camp.

I haven't chosen a camp yet. I'm not sure I'll ever choose a camp. There's a certain allure to learning to be me without a man.

"He wouldn't tell me," said Aggie.

Of course Anarchy hadn't told her *why*. Anarchy didn't just give out information. Inquiring minds had to poke and prod and sometimes beg before he said much of anything. "What did he say?"

"Just that he was cancelling your appointment."

"Nothing about a body?"

My housekeeper shook her head. Sort of. Between the tilt of her head and the dangle of her earring, she'd snagged herself on her kaftan. She moved her head closer to her shoulder and pulled the French hook out of her ear. The earring she left dangling from her shoulder. "A *dead* body?"

I put my purse down on the bombe chest in the front hall. "I'm afraid so. I found another one." That sounded truly awful. "Actually, a body found me."

"A *dead* body?" Aggie repeated. She sounded perturbed. She looked perturbed too. Her sproingy orange hair seemed to have lost some of its bounce, her brows drew together, and the tiny lines around her mouth looked like crevices.

If Aggie was perturbed, Mother would be apoplectic.

"Yes. A dead body."

"Where were you?" She tugged at the earring.

"The Gates of Hell."

"You? At a haunted house?"

I smoothed my skirt. What was so wrong with me going to a haunted house? "It's a long story."

Aggie yanked the earring free. "So you went to the Gates of Hell and found a body?"

"It fell on me."

"Someone having a heart attack?" She sounded almost hopeful.

"No. Murdered."

"Your mother is not going to like that." Aggie is a master of understatement. "Who was it?"

"A young man named Brooks Harney."

Aggie did not react.

She'd become so much a part of our lives that I sometimes forgot she'd only been with us less than five months. She didn't know the people who populated our pasts.

"Grace and his sister Camille used to be good friends." Aggie didn't need to know about Grace's schoolgirl crush on Robbie, Camille's other brother. "They were inseparable."

"What happened?"

"Camille's parents sent her to boarding school." Some of my disapproval must have leaked into my voice because Aggie tilted her head again. "After Brooks disappeared," I added.

She tsked. "He came back and now he's dead?"

"Yes."

Brngg, brngg.

"I'll get that." She hurried toward the kitchen and the ringing phone.

I glanced in the mirror. A few strands of hair had escaped my ponytail, and I smoothed them back into place. My earrings, discreet pearls, remained far from my shoulders and my sweater. I looked nothing like Aggie except for the worried wrinkles in my brow and the tight lines circling my mouth. I smoothed them with my thumb. At least I tried. The lines remained and my thumb came away covered in Chapstick.

"Libba is on the phone for you," Aggie called.

"I'll take it in the study."

I opened the door to Henry's study. The room was still very much his. Dark paneling and plaid upholstery. It needed redecorating. I would have done it months ago but sometimes Grace sat in here. It reminded her of her father. I sighed, sat behind Henry's enormous desk, and picked up the phone.

"You're never going to believe who asked me out." Most people started conversations with *hello* or *how are you*? Not my best friend Libba. She jumped in feet first and expected you to follow.

"Who?" We could play this game all day. It could be anyone from a Chiefs player to a scion. I grabbed a tissue from the tortoise-shell covered box and wiped off my thumb.

"Jay Fitzhugh."

A scion.

"Jay Fitzhugh?"

"You don't have to sound so surprised."

"Sorry. I mean, I'm not surprised." I was dumbfounded. Jay Fitzhugh seemed more of a walker than a player. He was a charming escort for older widows. The thought of him dating was...odd. "What did you say?"

"Yes."

Really? Aside from the widows, Jay seemed a bit dull for Libba's taste.

"Where are you going?"

"Dinner."

What could I say? Jay was gainfully employed—he ran the trust department of one of the larger banks in town. He didn't wear gold chains, shirts open to his navel, or a bad toupée. And, as far as I knew, he didn't secretly wear women's clothes or drink. Compared to the men Libba usually dated, he was a rock star. That he might prefer the company of men was a possibility best kept to myself. I twisted the phone cord around my ring finger.

"I chatted with him at your mother's gala," she said.

So the invitation to dinner hadn't come out of the blue. "Where's he taking you?"

"The American." Arguably one of the best restaurants in town.

"Do you like him?"

Silence ensued.

That silence spoke volumes. "Why are you going out with him?"

"Because I'm tired of spending my evenings watching television," she snapped.

Jay Fitzhugh was well-to-do, reasonably handsome, very charming, and single. If Libba wanted an evening out, who was I to cast a shadow? "I'm sorry, that didn't come out quite right. I think it's wonderful he asked you."

She sniffed. "What should I wear?"

"What about that new Sonia Rykiel dress? The blue one with the ribbons?"

"I suppose..."

"It suits you."

"Fine. What about you? What's new with you?"

Telling Libba I'd found another body—Brooks Harney's body—wasn't high on my list of things to do. "Nothing much. I played golf with Daddy."

"Liar."

"Pardon me? I'm just back from the course."

"That might be true but there's something else. I've known you for almost forty years. I can tell when something is bothering you. Spill."

"I saw Brooks Harney." No need to embellish with the state he was in.

"No kidding? I bet Genevieve's head is spinning like Linda Blair's." Genevieve Harney was blessed with unassailable wisdom which she shared generously. Brooks was the chink in her armor. A son who didn't turn out meant she'd failed. At least that failure had disappeared. For a time...

"I'm not sure Genevieve knows he's back."

"Where did you see him?"

"The Gates of Hell."

"Well, that's apropos. What did you talk about?"

"Not much. He was working there."

"Really? I imagine he's hanging around until he turns twenty-five."

"Oh?"

"Years ago, before Genevieve got quite so starchy, we had a couple of drinks. More than a couple. I think they were stingers..." Libba's voice faded with the memory of brandy and crème de menthe. "At any rate, she told me she worried that Brooks would run through his inheritance before he turned twenty-six. He gets his money from his grandfather on his twenty-fifth birthday."

Brooks wouldn't be getting any money. Brooks was dead.

"You ought to call Genevieve and tell her you saw him."

My stomach lurched left, ricocheted off my spleen, faded right, then settled somewhere south of my ovaries. Tell Genevieve I'd seen her son? Tell her he was dead?

Oh dear Lord.

"What are you wearing to the club Halloween party?" Libba had moved on.

I dragged my focus back to our conversation and said the first thing that popped into my head. "A clown suit."

"Fine," she huffed. "Be that way."

Truth was, on my summer trip with Grace, I'd found a vintage flapper gown that would make Mia Farrow weep with jealousy. "A flapper. Why do you ask?"

"No reason." Now she was lying.

I didn't feel up to calling her on it. "What about you? What are you wearing?"

"I'm going as Cher."

"Cher?"

"I'll have my hair straightened and wear a tight gown with spangles all over it."

"If the party is a dud you can always head down to The Jewel Box."

That comment was met with stony silence.

"Too soon?"

"I've got to go." Libba hung up on me.

Great. Now I'd have to apologize. But it wasn't as if Libba was the one who'd been carried out of the bar. Although it was her secretly-a-cross-dresser date who took us there. I returned the receiver to the cradle and stared at the phone.

I could call Marjorie. I should call Marjorie.

The doorbell saved me. I shot up from Henry's desk chair, hurried into the foyer, and opened the door.

Margaret Hamilton stood on the front stoop. Her arms were crossed over her chest and a pinched expression made her pointy face even less attractive.

We stared at each other.

"My cat is missing."

I'd guessed as much.

"Did that dog do something to him?"

That dog. Max. Where was he? I hid my hand behind my back and crossed my fingers. "I'm sure he hasn't been near Lucifer. He doesn't have much interest in cats." Max saved his hunting skills for squirrels and rabbits.

"Well, Lucifer is gone."

If I lived with Margaret, I'd leave too.

"I'll be sure and keep an eye out for him."

She narrowed her beady eyes. "Did you hear that Anne Landingham is moving?"

I hadn't. And I hoped it wasn't true.

"Her daughter is putting her in a home."

Was that a smile flirting with Margaret's lips?

I glanced at Mrs. Landingham's stately home. Surely her daughter could hire a nurse.

Having imparted her bad news, Margaret turned away.

Her turn coincided with Grace and Max's arrival at the bottom of the drive. Thank God Max didn't have Lucifer treed in the backyard.

While it's true that Margaret Hamilton doesn't like Max, it's also true that Max doesn't much care for her. His growl carried all the way up the drive and he pulled loose of Grace's hold and ran toward us with his leash trailing behind him.

Margaret shrieked.

I leapt past her, blocking her from my dog's muddy paws and bared teeth. "Max!"

He skidded to a stop.

A ridge of hair stood high on Max's back and his lack of barks suggested he meant business.

I grabbed his collar and pulled with all my might. "Thank you for stopping by. I'll let you know if we see Lucifer." If the woman had the sense God gave a slow-witted sheep, she'd hotfoot it off my front stoop.

Looking very much as if she was planning a new hex, one that made my hair fall out or my eyes bulge from my head, Margaret sidled past me and hurried down the drive.

"Sorry, Mom." Grace wore an expression unique to children who've been caught doing something they shouldn't.

"It wasn't your fault." I hauled Max into the house. "Bad dog."

Max didn't believe me—that or he didn't care. He trotted toward the kitchen as if he expected a biscuit for his efforts.

"I took him for a run."

"Up to the park?"

Grace nodded and her ponytail swung. "Four times around." A smile hovered near her lips and her eyes sparkled.

"What happened at the park?"

"Nothing." She spoke too quickly.

I cocked my head and waited.

"I saw Robbie Harney." Were her cheeks pink from her run or from the longstanding crush she'd had on her friend's older brother?

"Oh?"

"Camille will be home for Thanksgiving."

"You'll have to get together."

"He asked after you."

"Really?" Had Anarchy told the Harneys that Brooks had fallen into me? Surely he wouldn't have done that. Not until he found a body. It would be nice if he failed to ever mention me.

I glanced at my watch. It wasn't yet five o'clock. "It seems early for Robbie to be at the park."

Grace replied with a noncommittal grunt.

"Isn't he working?"

"For his dad."

"So he gets to leave early?"

"Lighten up, Mom. I'm gonna go shower."

She climbed the stairs with way too much spring in her step for someone who'd just run more than five miles.

Grace's crush on Robbie was cute when she was ten. Now that she was sixteen and leggy and lovely, I found it less adorable. I did some quick math. Robbie Harney was twenty-two. Completely inappropriate for my daughter.

"Grace," I called.

She stopped at the top of the stairs and looked over her shoulder.

"Thanks for getting Max out."

She looked...hopeful.

"You're still grounded."

She stuck out her tongue and disappeared down the hallway.

I followed Max into the kitchen.

He lay on the floor and watched Aggie chop something, looking every bit as hopeful as Grace just had. He too was sticking out his tongue. Well, maybe not sticking it out. His long, pink tongue lolled out of the side of his mouth.

I got an ice cube from the freezer and gave it to him. "Aggie..."

"You're going to need a Bundt cake." She jerked her chin toward the counter. There sat sugar, flour, eggs, butter, buttermilk (we had buttermilk?), a bottle of vanilla, and the Bundt pan. "I'll get started on it just as soon as I finish chopping the chicken—" Max looked up from his ice cube "—for your Cobb salad."

"Thank you."

She nodded and wiped her hands on the flowered apron that covered her kaftan.

Brngg, brngg.

"I'll get that." I picked up the phone. "Hello."

"Hello. Mrs. Russell?"

"Yes." I suddenly felt queasy.

"This is Robbie Harney calling for Grace."

No wonder I felt queasy.

"Robbie, what a nice surprise." It wasn't. "How are you?"

"Fine, thanks. And you?"

"Fine, fine." Aside from the fact that a college graduate was calling my still-in-high-school daughter, I was peachy.

"May I please speak to Grace?"

"I believe she's busy." I scratched my nose. "May I take a message?"

"I got home from the park and learned that Camille is coming in town this weekend. Would you please let her know? I'm sure my sister would love to see her." The churning in my stomach eased.

"I will, Robbie, but Grace is grounded." It didn't hurt to remind him just how young she was. "Perhaps Camille can come over here."

Seconds passed. "Camille would love that."

"I'll tell Grace. Thanks so much for calling."

I hung up the phone.

"Problem?" asked Aggie.

"I hope not. The boy—the man—who just called is twenty-two."

Aggie continued cutting chicken into perfect little cubes. "Too old for Grace."

I nodded.

"But he wasn't calling to ask her out?"

I had a suspicious mind. A cheating husband will do that to a woman. "He said his sister Camille is coming in town and wants to see Grace."

"Wait." Aggie's brow puckered and the even chop of her knife slowed. "That was the brother of the young man whose body you found?"

"It was. They ran into each other at the park today." I could have added that Grace had had a crush on him for going on eight years. I didn't. Instead I pinched the bridge of my nose.

"That's a situation that bears watching."

Truer words were never spoken.

Brngg, brngg.

"The damn thing's relentless." I snatched the receiver from the cradle. "Hello."

"Ellison, it's Anarchy."

And just like that the queasiness returned. "Yes?"

"We found the body."

I closed my eyes and propped myself up against the counter. "Where?"

"A couple of miles downriver. It looks as if whoever killed him tried to get rid of him in the Missouri. His body snagged on a limb."

Poor Brooks.

"I don't suppose you'd..." He cleared his throat. "It would be a terrific help if you'd take a look. I don't want to alarm his parents on the off chance it's not him."

He wanted *me* to identify the body?

The thought of identifying a dead, water-logged clown who might also be the son of someone I saw socially was not helping with the queasiness. Not one bit.

Viewing a dead body probably wouldn't help Robert or Genevieve Harney's stomachs either. "Of course."

"Thanks." That he sounded grateful didn't help with the queasiness. "I'll be there in thirty minutes to take you to the medical examiner's office." That *really* didn't help my stomach.

"Fine." I hung up the phone. I wasn't answering the blasted thing again anytime soon. "I need a bitters and soda."

"What's wrong?" asked Aggie.

"The police found a body. They want me to identify it."

She put down her knife.

"I'll get you that drink. You go change."

I looked down at my camel slacks and matching sweater. I was dressed for the golf course, not the morgue.

I trudged up the stairs to my bedroom and opened my closet door. What did one wear to identify a body? Black? Charcoal gray?

I changed into gray flannel slacks and a black turtleneck sweater then sat down at the vanity to brush my hair.

Three business cards sat next to perfume bottles and a brush set.

Tap, tap, tap.

"I have your drink." Aggie opened my bedroom door.

The cards were speckled with brown.

"Aggie, what are these?"

"They were in the pocket of the trench coat you asked me to take to the cleaners."

"They were?" I picked up the cards with the tips of my fingers and read the names on them. Charles Dix, a banker. John Phillips, an accountant. And Hunter Tafft. "How did they get there?" Last night was the first time it had been cool enough to wear that coat. The pockets had been empty.

Aggie put my hopefully-stomach-settling drink down on the vanity and peered over my shoulders. "That looks like blood."

She was right. The brown stains looked like blood. Brooks Harney's blood.

I knew where they'd come from. Brooks had slipped them into my pocket as he was dying.

I dropped them. The cards lay on the vanity's glass top, innocuous, harmless bits of paper.

Except they weren't. Those three little cards—well, at least one of them—meant a world of trouble.

FOUR

While it was true my father and Mr. Coffee were the only men I trusted, it was also true that Hunter Tafft was angling to join them.

Were it not for Anarchy Jones, I might've been dating Hunter on a regular basis—as opposed to our current irregular basis.

Having a dead man slip Hunter's card in my pocket was not good news.

The police called such things evidence.

But Hunter kept my secrets. Deep secrets. Dark secrets. Could I really just hand over his card to Anarchy?

I tapped the card with the tip of my nail. There was probably a completely reasonable explanation as to why Brooks had slid Hunter's card into my pocket. Until I knew what that reason was, I couldn't hand over the card. Could. Not.

I looked up from my study of blood-spattered business cards.

Aggie stood behind me, her face creased with worry.

"Would you please fetch a sandwich baggie?" I asked.

The lines creasing her forehead deepened, but she headed for the door without a word.

I sipped the bitters and soda she'd brought me. There's nothing like bitters for an upset stomach and mine had been churning since I got home. Churn wasn't a strong enough word. Especially now that I'd decided to conceal evidence.

Aggie returned and handed me the bag.

I picked up Charles Dix's card with the tips of my fingers and slipped it inside. Next John Phillips' card went into the bag.

Hunter's I left on the vanity. I stared at the thick card stock for a moment then pinched the seal.

Behind me, Aggie sighed.

"If anyone asks, there were two cards. Two." I held up two fingers.

Aggie nodded and the one earring she still wore bobbed. "He doesn't have anything to do with that young man's murder. I know it. You're doing the right thing."

Aggie's late husband worked for Hunter. When Al DeLucci got sick with cancer, Hunter covered his medical bills. Aggie was fiercely loyal to the man who'd helped her husband. She wasn't exactly objective. But hopefully she was right. I couldn't imagine a scenario where Hunter would kill Brooks, especially not dressed as a clown.

I took a gulp of bitters and soda. It did nothing to quell the rough seas in my stomach.

"You could do with some lipstick and maybe a little blush."

I glanced into the mirror. Aggie was right. Between the pallor of my skin and the black turtleneck I could pass for one of the corpses I was going to identify. I reached for a tube of lipstick, a soft coral shade.

Ding dong.

For an instant, both Aggie and I shifted our gazes to the card that still rested next to my perfume bottles. Hunter's card. Then our gazes met in the mirror.

"I'll call him and ask before I do anything."

She pursed her lips and nodded. "That'll be Detective Jones." She took a step toward the door. "I'll let him in. You put on some makeup."

When I descended the front stairs holding the sandwich baggie containing two business cards instead of three, Anarchy was waiting for me. Stubble darkened his cheeks and his slightly too long hair was mussed, as if he'd been running his fingers through it. "What's that?" His voice was rough, as if he hadn't slept since the last time I saw him.

"They were in the pocket of my coat. I think the clown put them there."

"Where's the coat?"

"Aggie took it to the cleaners this morning."

He scowled at me.

I scowled back. There was no way in this world or the next that I would have let him take my new coat into evidence. "Do you want the cards or not?"

He held out his hand. "Who do they belong to?"

"A banker and an accountant."

He frowned as if trying to discern why a clown needed financial advice.

"Brooks was a few weeks away from coming into a great deal of money." That explained Charles Dix's card. That even explained John Phillips' card. It didn't explain Hunter's.

"How much money?"

I walked over to the hall closet and pulled out the Burberry trench. "No idea. A great deal." Libba hadn't told me. And frankly, she probably didn't know. In my mind, a great deal ran to eight figures. Who knew what it meant for Libba?

I could find out exactly how much easily enough. Over cards. There was a wealth of knowledge available at the bridge table.

"Let me help you with that." Anarchy tucked the baggie holding the cards inside his jacket then took the trench coat from my hands and moved behind me.

I slid my arms into the sleeves.

For an instant his hands rested on my shoulders.

For an instant, guilt over hiding Hunter's card turned me to stone.

"Mom, where are you going?" Grace called from the top of the stairs.

"I'm going to take a look at something for Detective Jones. I'll be home in time for *Gunsmoke*."

"She'll be home in time for *Maude*."

Grace and I both gaped. That Anarchy knew when a show

about a middle-aged feminist aired boggled the mind—especially when that show ran in the same time-slot as Monday Night Football.

His coffee brown gaze shifted between the two of us and he shrugged. "It's my mother's favorite. I watch it with her when I visit."

I had no answer for that.

"Let's go." He ushered me toward the front door.

"Eat dinner without me." I stopped and looked back at Grace. "Robbie Harney called. Camille will be in town this weekend. Maybe she'd like to spend Halloween with us."

"About that..."

"You're grounded, Grace."

"You are so unfair."

Unfair? Unfair was getting murdered weeks before coming into money. "See you soon, dear."

Anarchy and I stepped outside and he helped me into his car.

"Who found him?" I asked.

"Harney? Someone on a barge spotted him. He was half out of the water."

Too bad I left my bitters and soda at home.

We drove in silence.

East. Farther east than I was accustomed to going. "Where exactly are we going?"

"Twenty-first between Campbell and Harrison."

An awful neighborhood. "Do you have your gun?"

He flashed me a grin. "Always."

We parked in a lot surrounded by a chain link fence topped with razor wire, and Anarchy escorted me inside. He signed us in with a bored attendant then led me deep into the building. Walls the color of congealed oatmeal, scuffed linoleum, and an oak chair with a missing spindle decorated the hallway.

Anarchy opened a door and the strong smell of cold stainless steel smacked me in the face. We stepped inside and the temperature dropped twenty degrees.

There were tables. On those tables lay bodies. On those bodies, hanging from the toes, were tags. I was sick of death. I blinked back tears and shifted my gaze to a wall.

The wall didn't help. It looked like a giant filing cabinet.

"Are you all right?" asked Anarchy.

"Let's just get this over with."

He rested his hand on the small of my back and propelled me forward until we reached the first table where he nodded at a man in a white coat.

The man pulled back the sheet.

I'd expected white makeup and a bulbous red nose.

I got blue-gray skin and sightless eyes.

All things being equal, I'd have preferred the nose.

Yes, I'd found bodies before. But those bodies had been...pink. Their flesh had looked like flesh not marble.

I clenched the icicles that used to be my fingers and studied the face. Thinner than I remembered. But the chiseled cheekbones, the divot in the center of his chin, the blond hair, somewhere between ripe wheat and spun gold, were all the same. The Harneys might have their problems—the Harneys definitely had their problems—but being unattractive wasn't one of them. I looked away. "It's him."

The pressure on my back increased. I leaned into it. Leaned into Anarchy.

"Thanks, Gus. Come on, let's get you out of here. You look pale."

He led me from the room and the reason for the chair in the hallway became apparent. I sank onto it.

"You're still pale."

Of course I was pale. My stomach was dancing a mambo, and I'd just left a room where bodies were filed in cabinets like last year's tax documents. "I'm fine."

"Let's get you a cup of coffee." That Anarchy Jones, he knew the way to a girl's heart.

* * *

Anarchy got me home in time for *Maude.*

I walked into the family room.

Max lifted his head from his paws, offered up one half-hearted wag of his stubby tail, then returned to his nap.

Grace gifted me a narrow-eyed stare then crossed her arms over her chest. Honey—running Max, being pleasant—hadn't worked to get her out of being grounded. Now it seemed as if she meant to try vinegar—being so unpleasant I'd want her out of the house.

I took a seat on the couch and looked at the television. Maude was insisting that Florida use the front door even though the back door was more convenient.

"Is your homework done?"

Grace rolled her eyes. "Humph."

"Tomorrow is market day. Is there anything special you'd like Aggie to pick up for dinner?"

The left corner of her upper lip curled. "Humph."

"Is there any chance you're going to speak to me this evening?"

The *humph* was there. Poised on Grace's lips. Apparent in the slits of her eyes. She wiped the word away with the back of her hand. "What did Detective Jones want?"

"I saw someone get stabbed last night. Detective Jones asked me to identify a body."

"Mom." The expression in her eyes changed—less Dirty Harry, more Benji. "Are you okay?"

"Of course I am."

"You saw this at the haunted house?"

I nodded.

"No wonder you grounded me."

"I grounded you because you missed curfew on a school night."

"Humph." This *humph* lacked the conviction of her earlier *hmphs*. Grace knew she deserved her punishment.

"I have calls to make." I rose from the couch.

"Humph."

Teenagers are such joys.

I climbed the stairs to my studio. Years ago, we converted the third floor ballroom into a place for me to paint. When we did it, neither Henry nor I ever dreamed my paintings would sell. They sold. Well. So well that I made more money than my husband. One might say the studio destroyed our marriage.

It was still my favorite room in the house. The place where I felt most centered, most *me*.

I plugged the phone into the jack and glanced at my watch. It was 9:20 in Akron. Too late to call? According to Mother it was impolite to call after nine. That belief never stopped her from calling me.

I dialed.

"Hello," said my brother-in-law, Greg.

We exchanged pleasantries then I asked, "May I please speak with Marjorie?"

"She's out, Ellison. Thea had a volleyball game."

Whew. That was one unpleasant conversation avoided tonight. "Would you tell her I called and ask her to call me?"

"Of course."

With those words, we ran out of things to say and hung up.

I stared at the phone for a moment, then my gaze shifted to some colored pencils left on the drawing table. Surely those needed to be put away before I called.

I returned the pencils to their box then picked up all the empty coffee cups and put them next to the door to be carried down to the kitchen. Next I straightened canvases. The clean brushes that had dried in a mason jar needed to be put away—never mind that they hadn't seen the inside of a drawer in weeks. They had to be put away *now*.

What else?

I straightened art books, ran a dust cloth over the surface of my drafting table, grabbed a broom, and swept the floor.

It was 8:57. There was no reason in the world I shouldn't call.

Not one.

Except...

I forced my index finger into the dial and turned.

He answered on the second ring. “Hello.”

“Hunter, it’s Ellison calling.”

“Ellison.” He made my name sound like warm brandy on a cold night.

I swallowed. “I’m sorry to call so late.”

“Don’t be silly. I’m happy to hear from you.” More warm brandy. A woman could get drunk just listening to him.

“I...that is to say...um, could we have coffee tomorrow morning?”

“Is there a problem?” Now he sounded concerned.

“Maybe. I found another body.” The words came so quickly they tripped over each other.

“Where? Do you need me to come now?”

“No!” I took a deep breath. “No. Tomorrow’s fine.”

“When did you find this body?”

“Last night.”

“Where were you?”

“The Gates of Hell.”

“You? A haunted house?”

“Yes.” I closed my eyes. “I found Brooks Harney.”

I waited for Hunter to offer me sympathy or make a soothing noise...and waited. I grabbed a charcoal pencil from a mason jar and a piece of paper and drew a line. A strong line, bold and distinctive. Another joined it. “Are you there?”

“Sorry. Just thinking. Why are you calling me now? You’re not a suspect?”

“No.” Thank God. I’ve been a murder suspect before, and I didn’t care to go through that ordeal ever again. But Hunter might be. I had to tell him. “Brooks slipped some business cards in my pocket before he died.”

“Oh?” His one word sounded wary.

“One of them was yours.”

Again I waited for Hunter to speak...and waited. I added more lines to my drawing. It was a face. Hunter's face.

"What did you do with it?" Warm brandy had cooled to the temperature of the morgue.

"It's sitting on my vanity."

"Who else knows?"

"Aggie." I added eyes to the face. Eyes that gave nothing away about the man inside.

"What other cards?"

"Charles Dix's and John Phillips'." I added dark slashes for eyebrows.

"How early can you meet in the morning?"

"Eight?"

"I'll be there."

I'd imagined a quiet conversation over a tiny table at my favorite patisserie, not Hunter in my kitchen. "Okay." I sounded squeaky. I cleared my throat and repeated, "Okay." Better. My voice sounded as if it belonged to a woman and not a five-year-old sucking on a helium balloon. "I'll see you then."

"I apologize for sounding curt. It's just—"

"Don't worry about it."

"I will worry about it. And I am sorry..." His voice trailed off. "I'll explain in the morning. Good night, Ellison." The warm brandy was back.

My pencil which had been drawing a severe mouth softened its opinion.

"Good night, Hunter."

I hung up the phone and stared at my drawing. It wasn't bad. Hunter Tafft. A man who kept other people's secrets.

What did it say about me that I could imagine Hunter as a murderer but not as a murderer dressed in a clown suit?

What did it say about Hunter?

FIVE

The sensible thing was to take a sleeping pill, set the alarm, and go to bed.

I did none of those things.

I paced. And fretted. And practically wore a path in the carpet in my bedroom.

The clock struck midnight before I donned a nightgown and one before I actually crawled into bed, so sure I wouldn't sleep that I didn't bother setting an alarm.

I slept.

I woke up and cracked a lid. Sunlight streamed into the bedroom. I rolled over and peered at the clock. 7:55.

Sweet nine-pound baby Jesus. Hunter was due at eight.

I levitated out of bed. My legs were running for the bathroom before my feet hit the floor. I brushed my teeth, washed my face, and scraped my hair back into a messy bun in record time.

The last vestige of summer color had faded from my skin, and I looked as wan as the zombies who wandered the Gates of Hell. I swiped bronzer across my cheeks and a soft pink across my lips.

Next, I pulled on a pair of jeans and a cashmere sweater and jammed my feet into loafers.

Finally, I strapped a watch that read eight o'clock onto my wrist.

Ding dong.

Hunter is nothing if not punctual, and I had to face him without coffee.

I hurried down the front stairs.

Max waited for me in the foyer, apparently curious to see who might be ringing the bell so early.

I opened the door.

If I was a last-second mess, Hunter was sartorial perfection—a navy suit with a subtle pinstripe, crisp white shirt, striped tie. And then there was his silver hair which shone like a newly minted dime.

"Good morning," I croaked. Then I grabbed Max's collar. Unchecked, my dog would sniff Hunter's crotch then rub dog hair all over the perfection of his suit.

Hunter didn't seem to care that nearing me meant the need for a lint brush. He stepped forward and dropped a kiss on my cheek. "Good morning. You look lovely." The man was a world-class liar.

"I—" I ran a suddenly damp palm down the side of my leg. "I overslept. Let's go start some coffee." I released Max.

He gave Hunter a perfunctory crotch sniff, wagged his tail, and trotted down the hall.

We followed.

God love Aggie. She was in the kitchen with Mr. Coffee and they were both brimming with good cheer. If she was surprised to see Hunter, she didn't show it. "Coffee?"

Aggie. Gem. The woman deserved a raise.

"Please." Hunter and I spoke in unison.

Aggie poured two mugs, put them on the counter, and pushed a white box my way. "I stopped at that French bakery you like and bought crescents."

Fresh croissants? The woman definitely deserved a raise.

She added two plates to the counter. "I'll be upstairs if you need me."

She disappeared in a swirl of celery green kaftan.

I opened the refrigerator and scanned the shelves. "I think we have marmalade and raspberry jam. Which would you prefer?"

"I've already eaten."

I hadn't. I grabbed the marmalade, turned to face the man in my kitchen, and steeled myself to tell him everything.

"Drink your coffee first."

He knew me well.

I put the marmalade on the counter next to the croissants, climbed on a stool, and wrapped my fingers around a steaming cup of heaven. I kid you not. The first sip of coffee in the morning is as close as mortals can come to walking with angels.

Hunter's lips may have quirked. His eyes may have twinkled. But he said nothing, letting me enjoy my moment.

It wasn't until after I'd drained my first cup and gone back for a second that he said, "Tell me what happened."

I resumed my perch on the stool, put a croissant on my plate and told him everything. I told him about the clowns, about Priscilla Owens and her great boots, about the empty room with the pool of blood, and about finding the business cards. "I had no idea they were there. Aggie found them."

"You gave Dix and Phillips' cards to Jones, but not mine?" His voice had that warm brandy tone to it again.

"Yes."

He took a step forward, caught a strand of my hair in his fingers, and studied it in the light. His lips thinned. "Don't take risks for me, Ellison. Don't lie to the police or hide business cards or—"

"You've done so much for me."

He dropped the strand of hair and moved his fingers to my cheek. His thumb ran the length of cheekbone.

My toes curled.

"I'd do all those things again in a heartbeat, but I don't want you to put yourself at risk."

Half of me—the half that was reading Gloria Steinem—wanted to argue that if he could keep my secrets I could keep his. That I was capable and strong and didn't need to be coddled. The other half—the half that Mother raised—wanted to melt into his arms and have him solve my problems.

He tilted my chin, leaned toward me, brushed his lips against mine.

Melting was looking pretty darned good.

Ding dong.

A look of annoyance flitted across his face and he pulled away. "Expecting someone?"

"No."

I stood, staggered just a bit—apparently my knees had gone weak—then pushed through the swinging door that led to the front hallway.

I reached the foyer and the bell rang again.

Someone was impatient.

I pulled open the door.

Mother stood on the front stoop.

I should have drunk my coffee faster. Mother before nine definitely required three cups. I stood gaping at her.

"Aren't you going to invite me in?"

Mother didn't need an invitation. She went where she wanted with the force of a mile-wide tornado.

"Of course. Good morning." I stepped away from the door and waved my hand at the foyer.

"I noticed Hunter's car is here."

"He stopped by for a cup of coffee on his way to work."

She beamed at me. A rarity. Then her eyes narrowed and her smile faded. "And you're wearing that?"

"Would you care for a cup of coffee, Mother? Hunter's in the kitchen."

The idea of Hunter in my kitchen returned the smile to her face. She brushed past me.

"Hunter, what a treat to see you. How have you been?" Mother slipped out of her coat and hung it on the back of one of the stools that surrounded the kitchen island. She meant to stay?

"Fine, thank you, Frances. How are you?"

Mother sighed, cut a quick glance my way, and sighed again. "The past several weeks have been difficult." Her meaning was clear. If only her daughter would stop finding bodies and settle down, everyone's lives would be much easier.

Hunter nodded as if he agreed. "I must say, that's a lovely sweater you're wearing. It matches your eyes."

Oh. Dear. Lord. Blech.

Mother and Hunter belonged to a mutual admiration society. I was not a member.

Mother patted her hair—her helmet—and sparkled at him. Then she somehow dragged her gaze away and inventoried my kitchen. Thanks to Aggie, not so much as a spoon was out of place.

"Who's the cake for?" Mother's eagle eye had landed on the Bundt cake covered by a clear Tupperware cake dome with a jaunty red handle.

"Um...the Harneys." This was going to get ugly.

She tilted her head slightly, like a mildly curious robin. "Why are you taking a cake to the Harneys?"

"Brooks died."

"He did? I didn't see anything in the paper. When?"

"Sunday night."

"Who told you?" She raised her brows as if she couldn't believe my gossip network might have scooped hers.

I should have stayed in bed. I should have insisted on the patisserie. I should have left Mother on the front stoop. I was capable. I was strong. I didn't need a man to solve my problems. I swallowed. "No one."

"No one?"

I ignored the urge to look at Hunter. Instead, I took a deep calming breath. "I found the body."

Mother was not given to swearing—especially not in front of the man she'd decided would be her next son-in-law—but desperate times. "Fudge."

Hunter guffawed then covered his mouth as if he could hide his laughter.

Mother glared at me. "How could you?"

I glared back. "It's not as if I went looking for him."

Her lips thinned. So did her eyes. The air around her head crackled with an impending storm.

Ding dong

"I'll get that." Call me a coward, but Mother looked as if she might hurl a lightning bolt at me.

I hurried out of the kitchen, down the hall, and into the foyer.

Max followed me.

He was a very smart dog.

I opened the door to Libba.

What was it? Get up unusually early day?

First Mother now Libba, women who made a habit of sleeping in unless they had a committee meeting, bridge game, tennis game, or, if it happened to be Thursday when women were allowed on the golf course in the morning, an early tee time. "What are you doing here?"

Libba blinked. "I saw the cars."

Hunter's Mercedes was parked in the circle drive in front of the stoop. Mother had parked her deVille right behind him. Libba's Porsche sat at the curb.

"I was just driving by..."

Liar, liar, pants on fire. Libba wore jeans and a crocheted poncho. She was not dressed for a committee meeting, bridge, tennis, or golf. She'd rolled out of bed and driven to my house.

"Oh?"

"I wanted to tell you about my date." That had the ring of truth.

"Come in."

Libba stepped inside.

"Mother's here," I warned. "And she's in a mood." *Mood* didn't cover Mother's current emotional state. There was a very real chance she'd kill me when I reentered the kitchen.

"I'm not afraid."

I was.

We took our time walking down the hallway.

I pushed open the kitchen door and Mother eyed Libba. "You're up early."

Pot. Kettle. Black. Speaking of which...why was Mother up?

"Mother, do you have a meeting?" She was dressed for one in a camel skirt and blue twin set with a silk scarf tied around her neck.

She glanced at her watch and scowled. "I do." That scowl spoke volumes. She'd much rather remain in my kitchen and explain my faults in excruciating detail. If I knew all my faults, and avoided them, I wouldn't endanger Hunter Tafft's interest in me. "Libba, you'll have to move your car."

"I parked on the street, Mrs. Walford."

Mother gathered her purse and her gloves off the counter, looked at her coat, and put them down again.

"Let me help you with that, Frances." Hunter lifted Mother's coat off the back of the stool and held it for her.

She slid her arms in the sleeves. "Thank you." Her voice redefined the term honeyed-tone. "See me to the door, Ellison."

Did I have to?

"Of course, Mother."

Together we walked into the foyer.

"You simply must stop finding bodies." She pulled on a glove. "Especially the bodies of people we know. People are going to start avoiding you...or blaming you."

"It's not as if I find bodies on purpose."

She sniffed. "Well, I've always believed attitude makes all the difference. If you decide not to find bodies, you won't."

If I decided chocolate cake had no calories, it wouldn't.

"What time is your meeting?" I glanced over my shoulder. "We left Hunter alone with Libba."

That more than anything else got Mother moving. "Go." She wagged her fingers, sending me back to the kitchen.

I walked toward the kitchen.

"Ellison." Mother's voice stopped me. "Perhaps we can omit telling anyone you found Brooks Harney."

That was fine by me. "Of course."

She managed a small, tight smile. "Go."

I went.

Libba and Hunter were waiting for me. So was Mr. Coffee and

he had something I needed. I bypassed my friend and the man who might—or might not—be my boyfriend and embraced the dependable fabulousness that is Mr. Coffee. I poured hot coffee into a mug, sipped, and sighed. "That sweater brings out the blue in your eyes."

Hunter shrugged.

"Mother adores you," I said.

"I enjoy her."

I did not—not today.

"Why are you up so early?" I asked Libba.

"I wanted to ask you...and it's simply wonderful that you're both here..." She studied the grain in the wood floor.

"What?"

"Jay and I had a nice time last night, and he mentioned he had four tickets to the ballet tonight. Would you join us?" She tried her best imploring look on me. I was impervious to that look. I'd seen it too often.

Unfortunately, Hunter was not as familiar with Libba's lexicon of expressions. "Of course we'll go." He fell for her please-it'll-be-fun-really-I-promise, hook, line, and sinker.

The ballet? Really?

"It sounds like fun," said Hunter.

No, it didn't.

"Wonderful!" Libba's smile lit the kitchen "How about dinner at the American before the performance? My treat."

As if two men, who'd probably stage an argument over the check, would ever let a woman near it.

I drove the short distance to the Harneys' home with the Bundt cake perched in the passenger seat. Aggie said it was lemon with caramel icing. My favorite.

I parked, carried the cake up the front walk, and rang the bell.

The October wind came in gusts, whipping leaves around my legs and blowing the last of Mother's concerns to the east. The

Harneys wouldn't blame me. After all, I came bearing cake, a sympathetic smile, and a genuine regret over the loss of their son.

Also, Brooks' death wasn't my fault.

Robbie Harney opened the door. "Mrs. Russell, hello." Like his brother, Robbie had been blessed with golden hair, chiseled cheekbones, and a strong jaw. He also possessed a charming smile. One he used now.

"Hello, Robbie." It took effort to balance concern and friendliness while hiding my dislike.

Robbie Harney had encouraged Grace's crush. And crushes are crushing.

He looked at the cake in my hands. "You heard."

"I did and I'm so sorry."

"Won't you come in?" He led me to the living room. The walls were painted a muted gold, the wingbacks were covered in a flame stitch fabric of the same gold along with delft blue, pine green, and a soft umber. That same umber covered matching sofas drowning in needlepoint pillows. Everything sat on a museum quality Ushak. The room should have felt warm and inviting. It didn't. It felt as cold and remote as the morgue.

"I'll put this—" he held up the cake "—in the kitchen and tell Mother you're here. Would you care for coffee?"

"Please."

He left me alone and I wandered over to a collection of four pastel portraits. Smiling babies all. Brooks, Robert, Camille and...

I'd forgotten about Chessie.

Brooks was the second child the Harneys had lost.

I searched my memory for the story and vague recollections surfaced. Genevieve had left the boys with their sister and there'd been an accident. The little girl had died. The details were lost. I'd have to ask Mother.

"Ellison."

I turned away from the portraits.

Genevieve Harney stood just inside the entrance. Her hair was perfect. Her dress was gray. Her eyes were dry.

"Genevieve, I'm so very sorry for your loss."

She stepped farther into the room. Her face was pale except for the apples of her cheeks. Those were a deep shade of rose. "It's kind of you to come. Please, have a seat."

I chose one of the flame stitched chairs.

Genevieve sat in the other. "Robbie is putting together some coffee for us." A grimace flitted across her face.

"I won't stay long. I just wanted to offer you my sympathies."

She stared at the hands clasped in her lap and nodded. "We hadn't seen him in years. I've been...I've been waiting for a call from the police since he left. He had problems." She looked up at me. The stark white of her skin and the dark material of her dress made her look otherworldly. Poor woman.

"It couldn't have been easy. Not knowing."

"This is going to sound awful, but at least now I know he's not suffering or living in some roach-infested hovel with the dregs of humanity doing Lord knows what for his next fix."

"Brooks was...never mind."

"What?"

Brooks had a job flirted with my lips, but I doubted knowing her son had turned his life around before he was murdered would ease Genevieve's pain. And was being a clown at a haunted house a job that would make Genevieve feel better about Brooks' last days? Doubtful. "Nothing."

Robbie appeared with a silver coffee service and saved me from having to explain.

"I'm so sorry about your brother, Robbie." I'd already told him once but it bore repeating.

Robbie grimaced. "I know it sounds harsh, but as far as I'm concerned, Brooks died a long time ago."

Genevieve made a sound—a tiny one—like a mouse sighing, and raised her hand to her throat.

"How did you find out?" Robbie asked. "We haven't told anyone or put anything in the paper."

"I saw him."

Genevieve leaned toward me. "Where?"

Given the circumstances, the Gates of Hell did not seem like a kind answer. "At a haunted house. I believe he was working there."

Genevieve sagged like a Raggedy Ann doll. "Working? At a haunted house?"

I knew I should have kept that to myself.

"And you saw him?"

I nodded, afraid to say anything else.

"What did he say?" asked Genevieve.

I should have kept my fool mouth closed.

"Coffee?" Robbie held out a cup to me.

I leaned forward and gratefully took the cup from him. The delicate china rattled in its saucer. I used my second hand to steady it. "Thank you."

He poured a second cup, stood, took it to his mother, and put it her hands. "You look as if you need this."

"Thank you, dear."

Genevieve's cup didn't shake or rattle. I looked at her more closely. Despite her Raggedy Ann impersonation, her eyes were still dry. Lord knew her hands were steady.

"We didn't speak." Brooks gasping my name right before he died did not count as conversation.

"What was he doing there?"

"He was one of the characters. He scared people."

Robbie threw his arm across the back of the sofa and crossed his ankle over his knee. The pose of a man at ease. "I bet he was good at that."

I wasn't buying Robbie's easy attitude. Despite his relaxed posture, he seemed tightly wound.

"If he was in town, why didn't he let us know?" Genevieve certainly sounded bereft. She even looked bereft with her gaze cast on the folded hands in her lap. So why did I get the impression she was simply saying the right words, the expected words? She leaned forward and picked up her coffee cup. Rock steady.

Robbie shifted as if the sofa cushion had grown sharp spikes.

"The last time you saw him you threatened to have him arrested."

The saucer in Genevieve's hand rattled then.

"No one blames you." An expression I didn't recognize flitted across Robbie's handsome young face. "He stole from us."

Ugh. I took a small sip of coffee. Burnt coffee. Double ugh. Obviously the Harneys hadn't met Mr. Coffee. I put the cup down on the coffee table. "I should be going."

"No! Please don't go. How did he look when you saw him?"

"He was in costume, Genevieve. I don't know."

"Costume?"

"He was dressed as a clown."

From the couch, Robbie coughed.

"He always loved clowns. Always." She too put down her coffee. Then she reached into the pocket of her dress, withdrew a linen handkerchief, and daubed her dry eyes. "We're having a small memorial service on Thursday. I hope you'll come."

How could I say no?

"I really should be going."

Robbie stood with insulting alacrity. "When you saw Brooks, you're sure he didn't say anything?"

My name and a plea for help. "I'm sure. Just hello."

"That's it?" Why did Robbie care so much about what his brother had said?

"At first, I didn't realize it was Brooks who was speaking to me. He was wearing a costume and face paint."

"That Brooks, what a clown." Rob's voice was harsh. With grief?

A single tear rolled down Genevieve's pale face.

I bent and kissed her cheek. "Let me know what time on Thursday." I turned to Robbie. "I'll see myself out."

I hurried to my car, climbed in, sat for a moment, and breathed air untainted by the Harneys' unhappy history.

SIX

That evening Hunter pulled his Mercedes up to the valet station in front of the American Restaurant at precisely six o'clock. The attendant stepped forward, opened the door, and helped me out of the car.

Libba and Jay Fitzhugh stood waiting inside the glass atrium. Jay glanced at his watch and his brow wrinkled. Oh, dear. If he was one of those on-time-is-late people, he and Libba were doomed before they started.

Hunter came around the car, took my arm, and escorted me in.

Libba and I hugged. Hunter and Jay shook hands. Hunter kissed Libba's cheek. Jay kissed mine. Hunter exclaimed over how lovely Libba looked. Jay did the same for me.

My friend looked at my dress, a black Diane von Furstenberg with a neckline that was—for me—low, and nodded her approval.

Libba wore a conservative—for her—dress with simple lines. Interesting. If Libba was willing to change the way she dressed and be on time, there had to be more to Fitzhugh than I originally thought.

The four of us took the elevator upstairs and the maître d', Maurice, met us at his desk. Behind him, the restaurant's ceilings soared in cathedral-like glory. "I have your table ready."

He led us down the first flight of stairs to a table that was half banquette seating (the banquette was a lovely rose velvet) and half chairs.

"I'd prefer a table by the window," said Jay.

The north side of the American was a wall of glass. On the other side lay the night and a spectacular view of downtown.

"That one there." Jay pointed to the last empty table next to the window.

"I'm sorry, Mr. Fitzhugh. That table is reserved."

Jay patted his suit coat as if searching for his wallet, seemingly certain that a twenty would make the maître d' lose a reservation.

"I wish I could make the change for you, Mr. Fitzhugh, but it's not possible."

Jay's brow wrinkled again. Lots of wrinkles. Wrinkles until he looked like a Shar-Pei. He found his wallet and withdrew a fifty.

A fifty? That seemed rather extravagant.

Maurice eyed Ulysses S. Grant and swallowed.

Jay added a smile and held the bill out. "That's my favorite table."

Maurice shoved his hands in his pockets and shook his head. "I wish I could."

Libba rested her hand on Jay's arm. "The food here is so marvelous I never notice the view."

"Fitzhugh, this table is one of their best," said Hunter

Jay's gaze traveled from Libba to Hunter to me.

"This table is perfect," I said. "Let's sit."

"If you're sure. Only the best for Libba." He pulled a chair away from the table. "Dear?"

Dear? Already?

Libba sat.

Hunter and I exchanged a look. Easy endearments were not a good sign. Also not a good sign? Losing a skirmish with a maître d'. Libba could do better.

I should have told Hunter ahead of time—just so he'd know what to expect. Libba had terrible taste in men. But people who live in glass houses shouldn't throw stones, and I'd married a man who made Libba's worst date ever look like a prince.

Hunter held my chair, I took my seat, then he and Jay joined us.

"Maurice, send over a bottle of Dom Perignon," said Jay. "We're celebrating."

"What are we celebrating?" Champagne gave me a headache.

Jay reached across the table and closed his fingers around Libba's hand. "We're celebrating the first of many wonderful evenings together."

Oh. That. Not if I could help it. Already there was something about him I didn't like. Libba's cross-dressing date who left me at a brawl was a better choice for her than a man who seemed head over heels after one date.

Maurice unfurled an elaborately folded napkin and allowed it to drift into Libba's lap. He repeated the operation for me. "I'll send a bottle right over."

A moment later, a waiter poured the Champagne into flutes. When we were all served, Jay raised his glass. "To beginnings."

We clinked our glasses and drank. Well, I pretended to drink.

Around us hummed the murmurs of polite conversations. The linen tablecloth was as white as fresh snow, the silverware gleamed, the bubbly—well, bubbled. The four of us articulate, educated adults looked for something to say.

Jay cleared his throat. "Did you see that Washington Post article?"

"Which one?" asked Hunter.

"The Federal Energy Administration says we'll never be free of our dependence on foreign oil." Jay reached over to the silver ice bucket placed next to our table and grabbed the Champagne bottle by the neck. He glanced at our nearly fully flutes then refilled his own. "If I were a chemical engineer, I'd be working on finding a substitute."

"Well, I wish you'd hurry. I'm not a fan of conservation, and I hate driving fifty-five on the highway. I think my car does too." Libba was probably right about her car. That Porsche could fly.

Jay pet Libba's hand. "Now, dear, just think of all the gasoline we'll save." He didn't stop there. He had facts about miles per gallon and emissions. He poured himself a third glass of

Champagne and told us about safety studies. After a few dull moments, I glanced around the crowded restaurant. The Fergusons sat three tables away. I caught Mary's eye and we exchanged smiles and nods. There was John Ballew with a woman whose back was to me. Libba would be better off dating him than Jay Fitzhugh—and John, recently divorced from a cheating wife, carried some serious baggage.

Finally, Jay ran out words.

The rest of us sat in numbed silence.

"I believe I'll have a scotch." Hunter looked around for a waiter.

I rested my hand on his arm. "A martini for me?"

"Not Champagne drinkers? More for Libba and me." He reached for the empty bottle.

Libba mouthed *Sorry*.

Jay seemed oblivious. "So, Tafft, how's the law business?"

"Steady."

"I heard a good one the other day."

"Oh?"

"What's the difference between a lawyer and a leech?"

Libba and I sat in itchy silence. Hunter merely looked polite.

"After you die, a leech stops sucking your blood." Jay laughed at his own joke. It was nice someone did.

Libba's streak of bad dates was intact—and enhanced. Jay Fitzhugh wasn't merely boring; he was a bore. A bore who couldn't hold his liquor.

A bore who turned his attention on me. "What about you, Ellison? Anything exciting happening in your world?" Did he have an artist joke he wanted to tell?

"I have a gallery opening in New York in late November."

"That's it?"

The polite mask that rested on Hunter's face slipped and for an instant he glared. "The gallery where Ellison is showing is one of the best in New York. Most artists would give their right arm to open there."

Jay shrugged. "Anything closer to home? What exciting things do you do besides paint?" The way he said exciting made it abundantly clear what he thought of my painting.

Exciting? I'd found Brooks Harney. That was exciting. But I wasn't about to tell Jay Fitzhugh about that. "Nothing."

Silence fell again.

Jay picked up his near empty Champagne flute. "What's the difference between a lawyer and a bucket of manure?"

Oh dear Lord. Another one?

Hunter didn't react. His polite mask didn't falter and his gentleman-at-ease posture didn't tighten.

He probably heard lawyer jokes all the time. I didn't. Something unexamined and imprudent made me speak. "Do you know Charles Dix?"

The glass in Jay's hand froze halfway to his lips. "Charlie? Sure. He works in my department." Jay tipped his head back, put his glass to his lips, and let the last drops of Champagne slide down his throat. "Why do you ask?"

"I came across his name the other day. I thought you were at the same bank."

Hunter raised a brow but said nothing.

"We are." Jay nodded. "Charlie's a good man, a good trust officer."

"So he's a trust officer?" It hadn't said that on his card.

"Has been for years. Are you looking to move your trusts?"

"No." I glanced at my watch. It couldn't be right. According to the Piaget on my wrist, only fifteen minutes had passed since we sat down. I forced a cheery tone into my voice. "If we're going to make the performance, we'd better order."

I sat at the kitchen counter nursing a cup of coffee and a headache. The headache I blamed on Jay Fitzhugh. He'd insisted we go out for a brief nightcap after the ballet.

I'd ordered a stinger in hopes of anesthetizing myself to his bad jokes and pontificating. One hadn't worked so I'd had two. Two stingers and we'd still made it home by eleven. Hunter had seen to that.

Now there was an elephant on the backstairs. I winced with each clack of its enormous feet against the hardwood.

The elephant appeared in the kitchen wearing boots we'd bought on our trip to Italy. "Good morning, Mom."

There was nothing good about it. "Good morning."

"You were out late."

"It wasn't my intent."

She opened the refrigerator door and stood there, surveying the shelves.

Max, who kept careful inventory of everything that went into and came out of the refrigerator, lifted his head from his paws. His stubby tail ventured a hopeful wag.

Grace reached into the fridge and withdrew yogurt, the butter dish, and a loaf of cinnamon raisin bread.

Raisins had no business defiling an innocent loaf of bread.

Apparently Max agreed; he returned his head to his paws with an aggrieved sigh.

Grace dropped two slices in the toaster and grabbed a spoon for her yogurt. "I heard something last night."

"Oh?"

She kept her back to me, waiting on her defiled toast. "I heard that Brooks Harney is dead."

I took an extra large sip of coffee and glanced at Mr. Coffee. He sat on the counter, his pot half-full, just waiting for me to ask him for more. "It's true." Then—I blame the lingering effects of brandy and crème de menthe—I added, "I took a Bundt cake yesterday."

"You did?" Grace cocked her head to one side. "No one knew until last night."

Damn stingers. "I did."

She turned and faced me. "How?"

"I found him. His was the body."

She shook her head and her ponytail swung like a metronome.

"He was fished out of the river."

"I found him before that. In the haunted house." Me and my big mouth.

Again the ponytail swung from side to side. "I was there and I didn't see him."

"He was hard to recognize." White pancake makeup, fuzzy hair, and a red nose can disguise anyone. "And when you were there, he wasn't dead." Ugh. I was supposed to be protecting Grace. She'd been exposed to enough death, enough murder. She didn't need to know the details, that I'd watched Brooks die.

"Why didn't you tell me about it?"

"I didn't want to upset you and—" I peered into my empty coffee cup. How had that happened? "— it's an active police investigation."

"How did the body get from the haunted house to the river?"

"That is a mystery for Anarchy to figure out." Not much of a mystery. The murderer had moved him. Finding out *why* he'd moved Brooks was the mystery.

Grace's toast popped, filling the kitchen with the mouth-wateringly delicious scent of warm cinnamon. Such a shame about those raisins. I rose from my stool and poured myself another cup of coffee.

Grace smeared butter across her toast. "I'd heard he came back a while ago."

"Really? From whom?"

"I don't know. Peggy?" She tilted her head, "No. Kim? I can't remember."

"I don't suppose it matters." Maybe it did matter. Maybe something he'd been doing had gotten him killed.

From outside came the unmistakable knocks of Aggie's VW bug settling in for the day.

"Sarah!" Grace pointed her butter knife at me. "It was Sarah."

"Who?"

"Sarah."

"I've never heard you mention a Sarah before." If I was

Mother, I'd ask after her people. Her father's name, her mother's. "Are you at school together?"

Grace nodded, setting her ponytail swinging in a new direction. "She's a year younger than me, but she's super smart. She's in our math class."

"How did she know Brooks?"

"I think her dad knew him."

"What's Sarah's last name?"

"Dix."

Dix? Questions tripped over each other on their way to my lips.

"How—"

Aggie bustled into the kitchen with the newspaper in one hand and a grocery sack in the other. "Good morning."

"Good morning, Aggie." Grace and I spoke as one.

Max yawned, rose to his paws, stretched then ambled over to Aggie and rubbed his head against her kaftan. An orange and black one today, presumably another outfit in honor of the coming holiday.

Aggie put the paper down on the counter in front of me and scratched behind his ears with her free hand. "It's a beautiful morning outside." She glanced at the clock on the wall. "Grace, shouldn't you be on your way to school?"

Grace looked at the clock as well. "Yikes!" She jammed half a slice of toast into her mouth.

"How did Sarah know about Brooks?" I asked.

"Ooks ame igh their ouse."

Oh dear Lord. I'd raised a cretin.

"Chew and swallow."

She did both. "Sorry, Mom. Brooks came by their house to see Sarah's dad. She was telling us about this super cute guy who showed up in her living room. She didn't realize we knew his sister." Grace jammed the rest of the toast in her mouth. "Otta owe. Igh, Omm. Igh, Akkie." She hefted her backpack onto her shoulder and disappeared out the back door.

"Have a good day," I called. The rest of my questions would have to wait until she came home.

Aggie unloaded what looked like the ingredients for stew from her bag.

I drank my coffee.

Brnng, brnng.

We both stared at the phone.

It wasn't yet eight. It had to be Libba. Or Mother. Or Daddy. I didn't much want to talk to any of them. Not without a couple of aspirin.

Aggie picked up the receiver. "Hello." She listened for a moment. "Let me see if she's up." She covered the mouthpiece with her hand.

Aggie. Gem. Deserved a raise.

"Who is it?" I whispered.

"Detective Jones. He'd like to speak with you. He says it's important." Her voice was barely audible.

What now? I nodded.

"One moment, detective. I hear her on the stairs."

She brought the receiver to me. Grace had stretched the cord to such lengths that, despite the distance, it sagged in the middle.

"Hello."

"Explain how Harney slipped those cards into your pocket."

No *hello*. No *good morning*. Something serious had happened.

My headache, which had been a tight band around my skull, tightened and thwacked me between the eyes. I pinched the bridge of my nose and closed my eyes. "Just a minute. Aggie, would you please get me some aspirin?"

I heard Aggie open a cabinet, shake a bottle of pills, and fill a glass with water.

When she put the glass on the counter in front of me, I opened my eyes and took the bottle from her hand.

I tossed back two aspirin and swallowed a mouthful of water.

"Ellison?" Anarchy didn't sound happy about waiting for a response.

I imagined myself back in the circus room of the Gates of Hell. "He said my name and I backed up into that popcorn machine with the head inside. The other clown stood just inside the doorway and watched. Then Brooks stumbled into me, and I realized the blood soaking his costume was real. After that, he slid down to the floor."

"And you didn't know about the cards?"

Dread mixed with the coffee and water in my stomach. My head pounded. "Not until Aggie found them. Why?"

"Charles Dix has been murdered."

SEVEN

Genevieve Harney had said she was planning a small memorial for Brooks. She'd understated things a bit.

The church was two-thirds full twenty minutes before the service.

I took a seat halfway down the nave and glanced around—discreetly.

The vast majority of those sitting in the pews were Genevieve and Robert's contemporaries. Where were Brooks' friends? I recognized only Warner West and Edward Dorsey.

"Move over."

I looked up at Mother. She prefers sitting on the aisle.

"I didn't know you were coming."

"Altar guild. Kate Alexander has too many guild members here and she doesn't need me. I swear that woman couldn't schedule her way out of a paper bag."

I didn't like Kate's chances for retaining her newfound volunteer position. Mother had an ousting set to her chin. But rather than going home and slipping off her pumps, she'd decided to attend the funeral. If I'd been asked to serve and found they didn't need me, I'd be gone in a New York minute.

"Are you going to move or not?"

I moved.

Mother surveyed the church. "It's a bigger crowd than I expected."

"Maybe Kate will need you after all." The guild manned the

reception after the service, replenishing coffee and making sure the cookie platters remained full.

Mother snorted.

The quiet such-a-tragedy murmur of mourners who weren't grieving surrounded us and we fell silent. I studied the backs of the heads in front of us.

"Is Grace coming?"

I nodded. My coat and purse rested next to me, saving her a seat. "She should be here any minute."

"Who is that?"

"Who?"

"Three rows in front of us. Middle of the pew. The woman with the coat."

Brown hair. A plaid coat in shades of plum and hunter green draped across her shoulders. The coat was envy inducing, but it wasn't much to go on.

"Why do you ask?"

"She turned her head and I thought I saw tears."

As if she could sense us talking about her, the woman turned and looked behind her. Our eyes met and I offered up a polite nod.

Mother was right. Priscilla's eyes were red-rimmed and the tip of her nose was pink and shiny. She'd been crying.

She jerked her head forward.

"Brooks' employer," I whispered. "Her name is Priscilla Owens."

"Why is she crying?"

"Brooks was killed at her haunted house. Maybe she feels guilty."

Mother sniffed. "I suppose it's nice of her to come."

"Is that seat taken?"

I looked up into hooded eyes, sharp cheekbones, and corkscrew curls pulled into a chignon and clenched my jaw to keep it from dropping.

"It's saved for my granddaughter."

Thank God Mother spoke. I certainly wasn't capable.

"What a pity. I would have loved to catch up, Ellison." The woman tilted her head and shrugged as if she actually regretted not sitting next to me.

The skin on my face stretched taut. This must be how it felt to have one too many facelifts. It took real effort to manufacture a polite smile.

The woman walked farther down the aisle then side-stepped into a pew.

Mother tsked. Probably because Kathleen was wearing a pantsuit. Yes, it was black. Yes, it looked as if it had been purchased from Bergdorf's. But one did not wear pants to funerals. Ever. "Who was that?" she demanded.

"Kathleen O'Malley."

"Who?"

Grace's arrival saved me from having to explain that Kathleen O'Malley was a dominatrix. She owned the club where my late husband and various women had—had done things I didn't care to imagine.

"Hi, Granna." Grace kissed Mother's upturned cheek, slipped past us, and took her seat.

I stared at the back of Kathleen's head.

What in the world was a dominatrix doing at Brooks' service?

"Mom, you're pale. Are you feeling all right?"

"I'm fine." I tore my gaze away from Kathleen and patted Grace's knee. "It's a bit warm in here."

"Stuffy." Grace shrugged out of her coat.

"Up there. On the left." A voice not modulated for mourning carried through the church. Mine was not the only head to turn.

A woman wearing impossibly high boots and an impossibly short skirt strode up the center aisle. Her face had that thin, mean look of a life lived hard. A man with a weak chin and an ill-fitting blazer with a sagging hem followed in her wake.

They passed us. The woman walked with enough determination in her steps for her straggly hair to bounce against her back. The man trailed two steps behind.

She slid into the first pew. The family pew. She claimed the aisle seat. The man stumbled past her.

"Who is that?" Mother used her scandalized voice. The one she usually saved for the discovery of illegitimate children and days when her daughter found a body.

"No idea."

"Well!" She glanced over her shoulder. "Where are the ushers?"

I too looked behind us. A full church—one that included Libba and Jay— gaped at the woman in the first pew but there wasn't an usher in sight.

There are people who say things like *someone has to do something*. Those are the people who look in vain for the ushers. Those are the people who clasp their hands in their laps and sit in disapproving silence as they imagine the Harneys' consternation at finding strangers in the family pew.

Mother is not one of those people. She stood. "I'll take care of this."

Next to me, Grace pulled her coat around her shoulders and sank lower in the pew.

Her teenage capacity for embarrassment was about to be tested.

Mother marched forward, an undefeated general faced with a middling challenge, and tapped the woman on the shoulder.

Straggly hair looked up at her.

Mother, her voice modulated for her surroundings, said something unintelligible.

The woman shook her head.

Annoyance flashed on Mother's face.

Grace's spine turned to jelly and she melted lower into the pew. "She's going to cause a scene."

Yes, she was. No woman in cheap boots and straggly hair could thwart Mother.

Perhaps Mother felt the weight of every soul in the church's stares. She whispered again.

Again the woman shook her head.

"Young woman, are you being deliberately obtuse?" A hush had fallen over the congregation and Mother's voice was discernable to at least the fifteenth row. Maybe farther. "This is the family pew."

"I'm family." Straggly Hair's voice carried farther than the fifteenth row. It filled the nave like a favorite hymn.

A collective whoosh of air and numerous gasps suggested every person in the church had heard her.

Next to me, Grace whispered, "Oh dear Lord."

My sentiments exactly.

Mother remained undaunted. She lowered her chin and raised a brow. A disbelieving expression is worth a thousand words.

"I'm Brooks' wife."

I glanced behind me. Faces registered shock or disapproval or glee. Libba looked sickened. Jay looked sick. In front of me, someone tittered. I suspected Kathleen O'Malley.

"Be that as it may—" Mother reclaimed my attention. She had not given up her look of disbelief "—do you think forcing yourself on your husband's family is a good idea?"

"They won't take my calls."

While Mother's intentions were good, she wasn't exactly saving the Harneys from embarrassment. Or Grace. Only the crown of my daughter's head was visible over the pew.

One of the missing ushers, Alan Hanes, hurried down the aisle. He stuck one finger inside his collar and pulled as if the cloth of his shirt had grown too tight. The other hand he kept clenched at his side. Poor man. If Mother couldn't dislodge the woman, no one could.

"I'm afraid you'll have to move," said Alan.

"No." The woman leaned back against the pew. "Brooks was my husband. My brother and I have every right to sit here."

The woman who'd strode down the aisle with a determined scowl hadn't looked remotely saddened over Brooks' death. Clearly she was here to embarrass the Harneys.

Alan looked toward the back of the church and jerked his head.

Two more ushers, Andrew King and Mark Wilbur, hurried toward the front pew.

"I'm not leaving."

Mother stepped back, ceding the battleground to the men.

As if sensing that her grandmother had left the fray, Grace raised her head just enough to see the front of the church. "This is awful," she whispered.

She wasn't wrong.

"What if she's telling the truth and they kick her out of her husband's funeral?"

Mark, a contracts attorney, leaned forward and whispered something in Mrs. Might-Be-A-Harney's ear.

Every soul in the church leaned with him, straining to hear what he said.

Mrs. Might-Be-A-Harney answered, her voice was too low to be heard.

They negotiated for another moment or two then Mark extended his hand.

The woman shook it, stood, and jerked her chin toward her brother, who had remained quiet.

The two retreated three rows, forcing Jane Addison to shift to the left or be sat upon.

Jane probably didn't mind. She had an eye for detail and she'd collect as much information as humanly possible. Cracker Jack ring? Singing off-key? Lack of tears? Jane would note all. Remember all. Then she'd dine out on all she'd noticed for weeks.

Mother returned to our pew. "Did you hear all that?"

"What Mark said? No." The rest I'd heard clearly. The people sitting in the last pew had heard it clearly. Angels in heaven had heard it clearly.

She shook her head, her mouth a grim line. "He agreed to pay her fifty dollars if she'd move."

Money well spent.

"One can't give that sort of person money. They'll simply come back for more." She might have continued but the organist started to play the Old Hundredth, the same hymn that had played at every funeral I'd ever attended.

The priest walked down the aisle and the Harney family followed. Robert looked remote. Then again, when didn't Robert look remote? Genevieve clutched a lace-edged handkerchief but her eyes were dry. Robbie—Grace sat up straighter as he approached—wore a properly saddened expression. Camille looked watery, as if she'd finally stopped crying but might begin again any moment.

Did they know about the woman who'd briefly occupied their pew? If so, they didn't acknowledge her. They filed in and took their seats without so much as a glance her way.

I'd been prepared for a lost sheep sermon. I wasn't disappointed. Reverend Stander can wax poetic about young life cut short.

Mother leaned her head toward me and whispered, "You'd think he'd get some new material."

You'd think.

It didn't much matter what the reverend said. All eyes were on the pew holding Brooks' supposed wife. She held the congregation's attention, not Reverend Stander. What would happen at the reception?

When the service ended the woman with the straggly hair rose before the Harneys. She walked down the aisle before the Harneys. Chances were good she lay in wait for the Harneys. Everyone else remained in their seats—on the edge of their seats—waiting for the Harney family to pass their pew before they rose.

The congregation rose in a rush. The church never emptied so quickly. Not a soul wanted to miss the meeting of Genevieve and Robert Harney with their purported daughter-in-law.

The crush in the undercroft was overwhelming. The Harney family stood against the back wall. Their daughter-in-law was nowhere in sight. Perhaps Mark's fifty had included skipping the reception.

The line to see the Harneys snaked through the crowded room. The cookie table was mobbed. Mother had disappeared. As had Grace—hopefully to see Camille then return to school. I waved at Libba who stood in line next to Jay as they waited to pay their respects.

"Good afternoon, Mrs. Russell." Warner West extended his hand.

"Warner, what a treat to see you." Our palms met briefly.

"It's quite a crowd."

"Indeed it is."

"Brooks and I were friends our whole lives." He shook his head sadly.

Warner wore a tailored navy suit and a Harvard tie. At some point, their lives had taken very different turns.

He glanced at me from beneath dark brows. "I heard you found him."

Good news travels fast. Good gossip positively flies. "I did."

"He was working a couple of jobs to pay tuition this semester. Next semester things were going to be easier."

I bet. A large inheritance would have kept him in school for as long as he wanted to go.

"What was he studying?" I asked.

"Psychology. He wanted to help troubled kids."

Poor Brooks. He really had been turning his life around. "Did you see him often?"

"No. We were both busy. I figured we'd have more time when Brooks didn't have to work so hard. He was off drugs—turning his life around."

"Where was he working besides the haunted house?"

"I don't know. He wouldn't say."

"Did you know about his wife?"

Warner pushed his hair away from his forehead. "I can't believe that. Even at his lowest, Brooks had better taste."

I knew nothing of Brooks' taste in women, but I did know women like that didn't crash funerals unless they were very sure of their positions. "Sometimes the people we think we know best surprise us." More like shock the hell out of us.

"That woman is just after money."

I didn't disagree. If she really was Brooks' wife, it was too bad for her that he'd died before he inherited. On the other hand, it was very lucky for the other beneficiaries.

"There's Ed Dorsey." Warner waved at someone in the crowd. "Would you please excuse me?"

"Of course."

He melted away and I surveyed the line to visit with the Harneys. It didn't look any shorter.

"I couldn't help overhearing." Kathleen O'Malley regarded me with her usual amused expression. One that said she found me vaguely pathetic.

"That's what happens when you eavesdrop."

Her mouth stretched in a grin. "The kitten has grown claws."

"Is there a safe word that will make you go away?"

"Meow."

Kathleen O'Malley was in my world and not some God-awful torture chamber. It was easy to stand up to her. "That's the best you've got?"

"Brooks Harney worked for me."

If she was hoping to elicit shock, I disappointed her. I've heard and seen much more shocking things since I first met her in her dungeon warehouse. "And?"

"I'd like to see his killer caught."

"What did he do for you?"

"Brooks felt a tremendous amount of guilt over something. He knew he deserved to be punished. He *liked* being punished." Her expression dared me to walk away.

I walked.

She caught my arm. "Wait. Brooks had a following." Kathleen glanced around the undercroft where people nibbled on cookies and sipped coffee out of paper cups. "Some of them are here. Tell that police detective."

Why did she always tell me more than I cared to know? I yanked my arm free, but I didn't walk away. "Brooks worked for you?"

"Just tell him."

"He'll want to talk to you."

She tossed her head as if she'd forgotten her hair was trapped in a chignon. "He'll have to find me first."

I couldn't quite wrap my head around Brooks Harney as a gigolo. "Brooks worked for you?" I asked again.

"As a submissive."

Curiosity. Cat. You'd think I'd learn my lesson.

"There are plenty of women who want to take charge." Her hooded eyes took my measure. "You might enjoy it."

Ugh. I had only myself to blame. I'd asked.

"As I said, Brooks liked the sadists. He wanted pain."

Covering my ears with my hands and singing *la-la-la* was not an option. I tried a freezing look instead.

"It was better for him than heroin."

I didn't argue. "Did you know about the wife?"

"Stormy?" She wrinkled her nose. "They weren't really married."

Stormy? Oh dear Lord. The way Stormy had forced her way into Brooks' service suggested—at least to me—that she was in possession of a marriage certificate.

"How long did Brooks work for you?"

"He started shortly after you came by the club."

My trip to Kathleen O'Malley's club of kinky horrors was something I'd just as soon forget. I'd paid one very short visit in June, discovered the depths of my husband's cheating, and made the decision to divorce him. He died before I got the chance.

A kewpie doll smile touched her crimson lips and her eyes narrowed slightly. "I miss Henry."

That made one of us.

The smile morphed into a pout. Had Mistress K really thought she could get a rise out of me over Henry? She crossed her arms. "Is that Priscilla Owens?" She jerked her chin toward the line where Priscilla stood.

"Yes."

"She looks exactly as Brooks described her."

"Oh?"

Kathleen's smile turned cruel. "They were having an affair."

"Priscilla and Brooks?" I considered that. Was Kathleen lying? One never knew with a dominatrix. If she was telling the truth, why had Priscilla pretended she didn't know Brooks was the clown?

EIGHT

After Brooks' service, I took refuge in my studio. With my legs curled beneath me in a battered leather club chair, I stared into space. The walls didn't offer much comfort, so I picked up a pad of paper and a charcoal pencil from the table next to the chair and sketched.

The weight of the charcoal against the paper's smooth surface calmed me. Dark lines on white. Control. Or at least the illusion of control. I emptied my mind and faces appeared.

Brooks Harney sightless in the morgue. His handsome features frozen by death.

Kathleen O'Malley with her hooded eyes and kewpie doll smile.

Priscilla Owens whose delicacy hid her strength.

Stormy, low-rent pretty with an ugly expression in her eyes.

Grace wearing the crestfallen expression of a girl in love with a boy who doesn't know she's alive. She looked so vulnerable I closed my eyes. How could I protect her from breaking her heart?

My pencil moved again. Robbie Harney with his classic good looks. Next to his face, I drew a stick with a hand wrapped around it. His face became a mask hiding Lord knew what.

Then came the murderous clown and the dark holes where his eyes should have been.

If I'd had the slightest inkling of what Charles Dix looked like, I would have drawn him too.

Tap, tap, tap.

"Come in," I called.

Aggie pushed open the door. She held a tray. "It's too late for coffee and too early for drinks. I brought both."

The tray held a carafe of coffee, two mugs, a pitcher of martinis, a jar of olives, and two glasses.

She put the tray down on the drafting table. "What'll it be?"

"A martini. But I shouldn't drink alone."

"I was hoping you'd say that." She put the tray down on the drafting table, added olives to the bottom of the glasses, filled them to the brim, and handed one to me. "Do you want to talk about it?"

"What?"

She pushed aside a stack of art books, plopped herself onto the edge of the chaise in a swirl of Halloween-themed (little skulls and jack-o-lanterns on a black background) kaftan and took a sip of her drink. "Whatever is bothering you."

The *no* that rose to my lips was automatic, formed by decades of keeping important things to myself. But I did want to talk about Brooks—my jaw ached with wanting to talk about Brooks. "I didn't just find his body. I saw him die." I took a large sip of dry martini and let the vodka work its magic. "How does a kid go that far off the rails? Was it something his parents did or didn't do?"

"You're worried about Grace?" With her sproingy hair, dangling earrings, and loud kaftans, it's easy to underestimate Aggie. A mistake. *Perceptive* is her middle name.

I wasn't alone in my concern. All parents worried about their kids. But my daughter had endured her father's murder, the death of friends, and a brutal peek behind the curtain of perversion. My jaw ached too much to answer. I nodded.

"That is wasted worry." She held up her glass and tipped it toward me. "Some people crumble under pressure. Grace gets stronger."

"She's still a girl and she's dealt with more this year than most people do in a lifetime."

"You are borrowing trouble. Grace is fine. Talk to her about all this. You'll see. Worry about something else."

"Like withholding evidence?"

Hunter's blood-spattered business card still sat on my vanity.

Of course Aggie knew what I was talking about. "Would you feel better if you'd turned over the card?"

"Hunter had nothing to do with that murder. I should have just given the card to Anarchy."

Aggie pursed her lips. "Of course he had nothing to do with that young man's death. But that police detective would have used the card as an excuse to harass Mr. Tafft."

That police detective instead of Detective Jones.

Like Mother, Aggie thinks I should fall into Hunter's strong arms and let him carry me off to a happy future.

I am not ready to let a man carry me anywhere, much less the future.

Aggie doesn't see it that way. Mother doesn't either. They've both said things that suggest they believe Anarchy is the impediment to my blissful future with Hunter.

How else could a woman resist Hunter's numerous charms?

"Who do you think killed him?" Aggie's question brought my attention back to her.

I looked up at the ceiling. No answers written there. "Brooks was turning his life around. I don't think he was killed over drugs."

Aggie waited for me to say more.

"Apparently he was some sort of gigolo for Kathleen O'Malley." So much better to use her real name than the one she used in her club—Mistress K. I shifted my gaze from the ceiling to Aggie. "And he was having an affair with the owner of the haunted house, Priscilla Owens."

Her eyes widened.

"How old is she?"

"At least fifteen years older than Brooks." I shifted my drawings to the floor and stretched my legs out on the ottoman. "If it were reversed and a forty-year-old man had an affair with a twenty-five-year-old woman we wouldn't think a thing of it."

"Those aren't the times we live in."

Too true. I crossed my ankles and took another sip of martini.

"Do you think the Owens woman found out about his other activities and killed him?"

Jealousy as a motive for murder? "Maybe." I swirled the clear liquid in my glass until the olive rose from the bottom. "There's also the money."

"I thought Brooks was broke."

"He was. But according to Libba, when he turned twenty-five he was to receive a distribution from his grandfather's trust."

"Who gets the money now that he's dead?" Aggie rose from the chaise, picked up the martini pitcher, and nodded at my near empty glass. "Do you want that topped off?"

"Please."

She poured. First in my glass then in her own.

Who got the money? Not the woman in the church. She couldn't inherit what Brooks didn't yet own.

"I don't know."

"But you suspect."

"If old Mr. Harney set up things like my grandfather did, Brooks would have received one-third of the principal. The remaining funds would have stayed in the trust until each of the remaining children turned twenty-five. With Brooks dead, the money will be split two ways as opposed to three. Unless..."

"Unless what?"

"Unless Brooks fathered a child."

"Did he?"

"Not that I know of."

Aggie rubbed her chin.

"How much money?"

"I'm not sure. Probably millions."

"So Brooks' siblings had a reason to want him dead."

Millions of reasons.

Camille had cried at Brooks' service. Robbie had not.

Camille was in Connecticut when Brooks was murdered.

But her brother—the young man Grace got dreamy-eyed over—was in town.

"Brooks had a checkered past. Anarchy probably has suspects we don't even know about."

"Ellison? Are you up there? I rang the bell and no one answered." Mother's voice carried up the stairs and through the door Aggie had left open.

Three o'clock in the afternoon and I'd had two martinis. "No."

"Very funny."

"Coffee," I whispered.

Aggie jumped into action. She poured coffee, handed me a mug, took the martini glasses, returned them to the tray, and covered the incriminating evidence with a tea towel that had somehow migrated to the third floor. All before Mother hit the top of the stairs.

We were being ridiculous. There was no reason two grown women shouldn't have a drink in the afternoon. Mother didn't make the rules in my house. If I wanted martinis for breakfast, I could have them. I straightened my spine. "You don't need to hide—" I caught sight of Mother's face and my voice died.

Mother looked grim. She had news.

But she made me wait. She scanned my studio, taking in the shabby, comfortable furniture, the easels, the blank canvases, the mason jars of paintbrushes, and the teetering stacks of art books. "I haven't been up here in years."

There was a reason for that. My studio was mine. A place free of toxic conversations and conflict.

She sniffed. "Do I smell alcohol?"

"I use it to clean my brushes."

Her gaze landed on the covered tray of martinis. "What's that?"

"A still life I've been working on. It's covered so nothing gets moved. What's happened?"

Her gaze shifted to Aggie and she smiled. Brightly.

Aggie knew Mother well enough to look worried.

"Mother?"

"That woman came back to the reception."

That woman? "Brooks' wife?"

"So she says." Mother shook her head at the sad state of the Harneys' affairs. "From the bleariness in her eyes and the state of her breath, I'd say she went to the parking lot after the service and drank before she came in." The tone of Mother's voice left no doubt as to her opinion of women who drank during the day.

My chair was suddenly less comfortable. I shifted my weight. "I'm sure that was very distressing."

"Poor Genevieve was beside herself. I told her you knew a private investigator who could look into the whole mess." Again Mother's laser-like gaze landed on Aggie.

If ever there was someone who didn't look like Sam Spade, it was Aggie. But her late husband had been a private investigator and Aggie had helped him. Now her eyes gleamed with interest.

Was she bored taking care of me and Grace?

"What exactly do you want me to find out?" she asked.

Mother looked down her nose. "We want you to prove Brooks didn't marry that woman."

"Does she have a marriage certificate?" Aggie asked.

"She says she does, but those things can be faked." Mother waved aside a pesky legal document with the flip of her hand.

"Who fakes marriage certificates?" It was the vodka talking. I have no other excuse.

Mother scowled at me. "Gold diggers." She glanced around the studio again, her gaze lingering on the towel-covered tray. "She also says she's pregnant. I'm sure she's lying. She's the type."

I spluttered on my coffee. If Brooks Harney was murdered for money, Stormy (who names their child Stormy?) was going to get herself killed and, if she was pregnant, her baby too.

When Aggie agreed to look into Stormy's claims, I had no idea she was signing me up as well. But Bess, Aggie's VW, wasn't always reliable and there was no way on earth I was letting her drive to the address Mother had given her for Stormy without a sure way out.

That's how I found myself in a part of town I'd never seen before at nine o'clock in the morning. "Remember, Aggie. I have a luncheon engagement at noon."

"This will be quick," she promised. Next she'd be selling me beachfront property in Montana.

Pre-fab 1940s houses lined a street where newly planted sweet gum trees spread their naked branches next to the stumps of diseased elms. Unlike my neighborhood where sprinklers kept the grass a vibrant green, the lawns were brown—where there were lawns.

Aggie and I parked in front of a house fronted by dirt, a broken bicycle, and flowerpots that looked as if they'd been empty since the Johnson administration.

We got out of my car and stared. The house boasted a narrow front porch with a broken rail, peeling paint, and shutters with missing slats that hung at drunken angles. And those were the good parts.

"Are you sure about this?" I asked.

"I've seen worse. It won't take long." Aggie set off down the short front walk.

I steeled myself for filth and followed her.

Aggie rapped her knuckles against a door that sounded as if it might be hollow.

"Just a minute," called a voice from inside the house.

Stormy opened the door and regarded us with narrowed eyes. "What do you want?"

"To talk," said Aggie. Well, that's what Aggie wanted. I wanted to get in my car and drive away. "I'm Aggie DeLucci and this is my associate." Her associate? "The Harneys sent us. Can we come in?"

Stormy studied us for a moment—Aggie's printed kaftan, the matching dangly earrings, and the heavy beads around her neck. And me, wearing slacks, a sweater, and no jewelry per Aggie's instructions.

Apparently we passed muster. Stormy opened the door farther then stepped back.

If the outside of Stormy's house was chaos the inside was...not. We entered directly into a small living room. It was neat. It was clean. It was pleasant. "Do you want anything to drink?" she asked.

"No, thank you," I replied.

"Come on in the kitchen. I was just making coffee."

We followed her into a kitchen populated by old appliances, worn linoleum, a small table covered with a cheery oilcloth, four mismatched chairs, and Mr. Coffee. Like the living room, it was spotlessly clean. "Have a seat." She waved toward the chairs.

Without makeup and her high-heeled boots, Stormy looked younger. Softer. Except for her eyes. Her eyes retained the wary look of a woman who expects the worst from the world. A woman who could give as good as she got.

"You want to know about me and Brooks."

Aggie nodded.

"I figured they'd send somebody. I expected a suit."

"You got me," said Aggie.

And me. But I wasn't talking.

Stormy poured herself a cup of coffee and joined us at the table. "Brooks and me, we met in L.A." She stood, opened a drawer and withdrew a pack of cigarettes and a lighter. She brought them back to the table, looked at its clean surface, and stood again. "Let me grab an ashtray. I'll be right back."

Stormy returned with a piece of harvest-gold hued pottery. She put it on the table, shook a cigarette out of the pack, and lit up. Then she sank back into her chair. "Better. Like I said, we met in L.A."

"What was Brooks doing there?" Aggie asked.

"He was a good-looking man. He thought maybe he could break into movies." She shook her head. "The junk got in the way."

The junk? I raised my brows.

Aggie mouthed *heroin*.

Oh. I folded my hands in my lap.

Aggie leaned her arms on the table. "And you? What were you doing in Los Angeles?"

Stormy breathed smoke deep into her lungs and exhaled plumes through her nose. "Born there. I had no illusions about making it in the movies." She took a sip of coffee and knocked the ash off her cigarette. "Brooks—Brooks was sure he'd be a star. And he was fun to party with. He told me if we could hang on until he turned twenty-five, we could party wherever we wanted, however we wanted, he could even finance his own film."

Aggie sat back in her chair. "You got married."

Stormy nodded. "It was his idea. He was bored one day, so he borrowed a car and we drove to Vegas."

"When was that?"

"July of 1972. I've got a copy of the certificate. I'm not lying."

"I didn't think you were," said Aggie. "What happened after you got married?"

Stormy took another drag on the cigarette. "You know when love makes you believe anything is possible?" Her lip curled at the corner. "We decided to get clean." She leaned her head back and blew smoke at the ceiling. "We tried hard. Brooks actually made it to a handful of auditions. He even got cast."

"In a movie?" I asked.

"Yes, in a movie." She shook her head as if I were hopelessly stupid. "A porno."

Oh dear Lord.

She shook her head again. This time with a tilt to her chin that suggested regret. "He met someone on set."

"A woman?"

"Yes, a woman." The hopelessly stupid headshake returned. "A domme. Brooks found kinky sex and forgot about me."

"Forgot about you?" asked Aggie.

"He actually got clean. Stayed clean. He told me if I didn't stop using he'd leave me." Another drag. "He left."

"How did you know he'd come back to Kansas City?"

"He'd check in on me from time to time. He told me he was coming back here."

"When was that?"

"March? April?"

"And you followed him." Aggie sounded sympathetic.

"There wasn't anything for me in L.A. I figured after Brooks got his money, he'd give me some." She crushed her cigarette against the bottom of the ashtray. "I tracked him down and he told me if I didn't get clean he'd divorce me. He'd left me once. I knew he meant it."

She glared at me. Why me? Aggie was the one asking the questions.

"Do you have any idea how hard it is to get off junk?" Stormy's eyes narrowed to slits as if I was personally responsible for the degree of difficulty.

I shook my head.

"It sucks. But I did it. And I told Brooks. Do you know what he did?"

"No." My voice was barely a whisper.

"He kissed me on the forehead and told me he was going to divorce me anyway." She hit the cigarette packet against the table with such force that a cigarette leapt out. She caught it then wiped under her left eye with the back of her hand. "I did it for him and he didn't care about me at all."

"He cared enough to want to see you off drugs."

She sneered. "So he walks away with his dominatrix friend and I'm left with nothing? I am still his wife. His widow. I am entitled to that inheritance."

"Brooks didn't have any money. Not yet." My tone was soothing—at least that was what I was going for. "You can't inherit what he didn't own."

"Of course he owned that money. He just had to wait until he was twenty-five to spend it."

"No." It was my turn to stare at the ceiling. "That's not how it works. The trust owns the money."

"You're lying. His family doesn't want me to have it."

If Brooks had died after twenty-five, she'd be absolutely right. Genevieve Harney would have moved heaven and earth to keep

Stormy's mitts off family money. But he'd died before twenty-five. "I'm sorry. It's the truth."

Aggie and I exchanged a glance. Was she thinking what I was thinking? Believing as she did, that she'd inherit a fortune, Stormy had a motive for murder.

"Where's your brother" I asked. Could the man at the memorial service have been the second clown?

"Work. He's got a job at a gas station." She lit yet another cigarette.

"You're pregnant?" asked Aggie.

"With Brooks' baby." Stormy took a long drag on her cigarette.

"You do know the Harneys will insist on a paternity test?" Aggie sounded as if the Harney family was being completely unreasonable. She sounded as if she was on Stormy's side.

Stormy wasn't fooled. The hardness that never left her eyes spread to the rest of her face. "Are you calling me a liar?" She pushed away from the table and pointed her lit cigarette at us. "You should leave."

We rose from the table.

Stormy waved her cigarette at us. "You tell Brooks' family I'm not going away. You tell them they owe me. Unless they pay up, I'll make sure every movie theatre in town screens their precious Brooks' porno."

She wanted me to tell Genevieve Harney that her son had appeared in...I shuddered.

"So high and mighty. You tell 'em."

Despite her colorful kaftan and corkscrew curls, Aggie looked sterner than a hanging judge. "Just so we're clear, you will release a movie that will embarrass the Harneys unless they pay you?"

"I just said that."

"You do realize that's blackmail? And that it's against the law?"

"Get out." Stormy pointed toward the door.

"They will prosecute." Aggie's voice was cold as death.

"Out!"

Aggie and I left.

My car started without incident and we sped away. “How much will it cost to fix Bess?” I asked.

“Why?”

“Whatever it is, I’ll pay it. I don’t want to drive you to any more interviews.”

“That?” Aggie raised her brows. “That was nothing. Just wait till I find the dominatrix friend.”

As long as I didn’t have to ask Kathleen O’Malley who the friend was...

NINE

I met Libba for lunch at Trader Vic's. Since she'd discovered the restaurant floated gardenias in the Mai Tais, it was hard to get her to go anyplace else.

Not that I was complaining.

Their crab rangoon was better than sex—at least any sex I'd ever had.

She waited for me at a table beneath several Maori tikis. An outrigger hung above her.

We kissed the air next to each other's cheeks.

"What a fabulous sweater," she said. She wasn't wrong. I wore a Missoni knit I'd bought on my summer trip through Europe. Black and white with gold accents.

"That's a gorgeous dress."

Libba twisted her hips and the hem swirled around her knees. "Isn't it? I picked it up at Swanson's."

The pleasantries taken care of, we sat.

"What did you think?" she asked.

She meant what did I think about Jay. I'd known that question was coming and had spent the drive to Crown Center crafting an answer. "Was Jay nervous?"

Libba tilted her head to the side. "No. Why?"

He'd drunk too much and bored us half to tears. "He told lawyer jokes to a lawyer."

"So?"

"Would he tell Polish jokes to a Pole?"

A waiter saved her from answering. "May I bring you a drink?"

"An Arnold Palmer." I looked up at him. "Heavy on the tea, easy on the lemonade."

"And a pupu platter," added Libba. Yeah! Crab rangoon.

The waiter made a note on his pad. "I'll have that right out for you."

"So you didn't like him?" Libba sounded crestfallen.

"It's not that I didn't like him." I didn't. "It's that he's so different from the men you usually date." Libba's previous bad dates had at least been fun.

Libba leaned toward me. "Different is good."

"It can be." Not in this case.

"Trust me on this." A Cheshire cat grin lit her face. "Different is good."

"You didn't." Did I sound as scandalized as I felt?

The continued curl of her lip was an admission.

"You barely know the man."

"I know him better now." She twisted her neck, stretching, then added a satisfied sigh. "We weren't ready to call it a night after you and Hunter went home. So we went back to his place." Libba took a sip of whatever she was drinking. "He lives in a penthouse on the Plaza. The view is amazing."

"You didn't go up there for the view."

"No." She looked at the table to the left where a couple held hands. Their fingers met near the salt shaker and the woman had a gardenia tucked in her hair. Then Libba looked at the table to the right where two men in suits ate Asian spareribs and drank martinis. She leaned forward. "He has—" her voice was barely a whisper "—toys."

"Toys?" I spoke—squeaked—loud enough for the businessmen to look up from their meals. I lowered my voice and repeated, "Toys?"

Libba nodded and a becoming pink colored her cheeks.

What kind of toys? My husband had developed a taste for toys. At least that's what he called his whips and handcuffs and—I closed my eyes.

"He's taking me to the club Halloween party tonight. You need to give him another chance. I want you to like him."

Toys? And I had to see him knowing that? Somehow I kept the corner of my lip from curling. What people did behind closed doors was none of my business. But...toys? "If you like him, I like him." I clasped my hands and ignored the itch that plagued the end of my nose whenever I lied.

The waiter brought my drink and I glanced around the crowded restaurant. I didn't know a soul. I was accustomed to dining in places where I knew at least half of those seated. Anonymity was a treat.

Especially when Libba said, "You should think about doing it again."

I choked on my Arnold Palmer. It? No, thank you. I had crab rangoon to keep me happy. I scowled at her.

"I mean it, Ellison. How long has it been?"

Years. Where was the waiter with that pupu platter? "None of your business."

"That long?"

"Drop it, Libba."

My voice must have held an edge because she changed the subject. "That was quite a service yesterday." She shook her head. "Poor Genevieve. I wouldn't wish that on anyone."

"Her son's death or Stormy?"

"Either."

I knew Genevieve because our daughters had been in school together. If not for Grace and Camille, the ten-year difference in our ages would have kept us casual acquaintances. "How did you know her?"

"I sat on a Junior League committee she chaired. Years ago. She had to resign when her daughter died."

"And you stayed friends?"

"No."

"Then why were you at the funeral?"

"Jay is their trust officer. He asked me to go with him."

I took a large sip of Arnold Palmer rather than comment on that.

"We were going to ask you to join us for luncheon afterward but we couldn't find you."

A small mercy. For me, Jay was best in small doses. I changed the subject. "Do you remember what happened to Chessie Harney? I didn't know Genevieve and Robert then, and I can't remember the details."

Libba tilted her head and caught her chin between her pointer finger and her thumb. "It was winter. And Genevieve had to run an errand. A quick one. Rather than bundle all three kids into their coats and hats and mittens and boots, she put Brooks in charge."

"How old was he?"

"Seven? Maybe six. I'm not sure."

I did the math—not my strong suit. If Brooks was seven, then Robbie had been four and Chessie just a baby, not even one. "She left a seven-year-old in charge?" Judgment crept into my voice.

"She thought she'd be gone for five minutes, but she got stuck in a snow drift."

"How long was she gone?"

"A lot longer than five minutes. When she got home, Chessie was dead."

When Grace was a baby, the thought of something happening to her had kept me up at night. On occasion, I still spent hours staring at a dark ceiling, worrying. "What happened?"

"Apparently Chessie woke up from her nap and climbed out of her crib. She fell down the stairs." Libba stared into her iced tea. "Of course, everyone blamed Genevieve."

As well they should.

"She blamed Brooks."

Was that the sin that Brooks spent his life trying to atone for? His sister's death? He'd been seven. The blame lay squarely on Genevieve's shoulders for leaving a seven-year-old in charge.

The waiter arrived and put the pupu platter down in the center of the table.

"Stay away from the crab rangoon." I swatted Libba's hand away. "It's all mine."

When I got home, full of crab rangoon and Dungeness crab toast (because nothing says Pacific cuisine like crab pulled from the north Atlantic), Anarchy's Gran Torino was parked in my driveway.

Not stopping, driving to the country club, the grocery store, or a quick shopping trip on the Plaza, would have been cowardly. It was also incredibly tempting. Nothing good ever came from one of Anarchy's unexpected visits.

I'd given him two blood-spattered business cards.

What if he was here to tell me that John Phillips was dead too?

I parked, got out of my car, and walked to the front door.

It opened before I had a chance to dig for my keys.

Aggie stood on the other side. Her cheeks were red. Her hair seemed to spring from her head with extra verve. Her eyes snapped.

Uh-oh.

"What's wrong?" I asked.

"Detective Jones—" she twisted his name into an expletive "—is here to see you."

"Are you all right?" I'd never seen Aggie angry before. She was a bit frightening.

"Fine. He's in the kitchen." She marched up the front stairs, each step, on each tread, echoing through the foyer. Quite something since a thick Oriental runner covered the wood.

I shuffled down the hallway to the kitchen. What had Anarchy said to Aggie? I cracked the swinging door and peeked inside.

Anarchy paced in front of the counter. His hair was messy as if he'd just run his fingers through it in frustration. The space between his brows was furrowed. His mouth he held in a grim line.

Confrontation made my stomach tighten like a fist. My stomach was currently full of seafood and Arnold Palmers. Maybe I should come back later...

Too late. He spotted me and the grim line of his mouth thinned even more.

I pushed open the door and pretended I hadn't noticed he was incandescently angry. "What a nice surprise."

"Ellison." His voice rolled like thunder during a summer storm.

"I've just been lunching with Libba." Not that he cared.

His hands were fisted, the knuckles white.

"Did Aggie offer you anything to drink? I can make coffee?"

He seemed to vibrate with strong emotion. "What the hell were you thinking?"

When? "Pardon me?"

"You went to see Brooks Harney's widow!"

Oh, that. "I drove Aggie."

"You went inside with her."

Had Grace been with me, she would have described the neighborhood as sketchy. I would have agreed with her. "It didn't seem particularly safe to wait in the car."

"It wasn't safe for you to be there at all!"

"As you can see, I made it home just fine. So did Aggie."

"What were you doing there?"

"We wanted to find out if Brooks and Stormy were really married."

To say Anarchy scowled doesn't even approach a description of the look he gave me. Laser eyes. Hewn cheeks. Thinned lips. And his brows a straight, unforgiving line across his forehead. "You were meddling." His voice matched his expression.

"I most certainly was not. Genevieve Harney asked Aggie to go and I could hardly let her take Bess."

"Who. Is. Bess?"

"Aggie's car."

He leaned against the counter and his fingers gripped the edge so tightly it was a wonder the tiles didn't crumble to dust.

"Bess isn't exactly reliable," I explained. He stared at me as if I were speaking gibberish and not perfectly phrased English. "I didn't want Aggie to get stranded if Bess wouldn't start. Sometimes she doesn't. Start. The car. Not Aggie."

"Did it occur to you that Stormy might have something to do with Brooks' death? That you might have been paying a house call to a murderer?"

"The second clown was definitely a man."

"Stormy has a brother."

It's hard to argue with facts. I went to the fridge, helped myself to a can of Tab, turned and asked, "Are you sure you don't want anything?"

Anarchy growled.

I turned my back on him, pulled a glass from the cabinet, and filled it with ice from the freezer.

Behind me a volcano rumbled.

I reached back into the fridge for a wedge of lime.

"You could have been hurt!"

"I wasn't."

"Luckily."

"You seem to think I'm incapable of taking care of myself."

"How many times have you been hospitalized since we met?"

That was too much. I slammed the refrigerator door. And cracked the glass down on the counter with such force it was a wonder it didn't shatter. I was more gentle with the Tab. With my hands free, I crossed my arms. "It is not your job to take care of me."

He closed the space between us in one enormous stride. His hands circled my upper arms. Tightly.

"Do you have any idea what it does to me when I hear you've been hurt?"

My mouth went too dry to speak. Probably just as well since my mind went blank.

"Do you?"

Somehow I moved my chin from side to side.

"My heart stops, the ground beneath me gives way, and all I can think of is getting to your side."

Tiny flecks of gold glinted in Anarchy's brown eyes. Stubble darkened his cheeks. A vein on the side of his neck throbbed.

Details are important. Details keep foolish women from melting into puddles on the kitchen floor.

His grip on my arms tightened. "You cannot put yourself in danger. I won't allow it."

Somewhere deep within me a tiny spark of annoyance flamed. Who was Anarchy Jones to tell me what I could and couldn't do? Every man I knew from my father to Anarchy seemed to think I needed my decisions made for me.

I didn't.

The spark inside me burned brighter. I wasn't some helpless damsel in distress. And Anarchy wasn't a knight come to save me. Nope. He was a man who thought me incapable of saving myself.

"I mean it, Ellison. You just can't."

The spark took hold and anger burned through my veins. "I didn't ask you to worry about me."

"How could I not?"

"I'm not some helpless ninny."

Anarchy blinked. And for a half-second confusion replaced grim resolve on his face. "I didn't say you were."

"As good as." I pulled against his grip on my arms. I might as well have tried to pull free of the earth's gravitational pull.

"You're deliberately taking things the wrong way."

I was not. "How many times have you been hospitalized since we met?" I mimicked. He'd said it. He couldn't deny it.

"Dammit. I just want you safe." He pulled me against his chest and kissed me. A claiming kiss. Hard. Demanding. More than I was ready for. But with one expert swipe of his tongue he eradicated all my objections, all my common sense. His kiss melted bone and good intentions.

Anarchy had ignored the electricity between us in the parking lot of the haunted house. He wasn't ignoring it now. The air around us hummed with need and desire and passion.

He released my arms, wrapping me in an iron embrace.

My arms—traitors—snaked around his neck. My body, quite of its own accord, pressed against his.

"Mom, I'm home."

I jumped away from Anarchy as if he was an overflowing tub of scalding water. Scalding was right. With one kiss he'd managed to burn away all my resolve.

Grace stood at the back door with Max's leash in her hand. "Um...sorry. I didn't mean to interrupt."

Max grumbled his agreement.

"You didn't interrupt." My nose itched like hell and my breath—I couldn't quite catch it. "Detective Jones was just leaving."

"Are you sure?" Grace puckered her face—lips, nose, brow. "It looked like an interruption."

I'd deal with her sass later. And—I narrowed my eyes—what was she doing wearing makeup on a run? Had she hoped to see Robbie Harney again?

She bent and unhooked Max's leash.

Free, he trotted across the kitchen and positioned himself between Anarchy and me.

I scratched behind Max's ears with a shaking hand, grateful that his body separated me from Anarchy. "Grace will see you out."

Anarchy's lips thinned. Grace's brows rose. I gave Max a final pat and poured Tab over melting ice with a hand that still shook.

Aggie's feet on the back steps alerted us to her arrival. She pushed open the door and regarded us all—my no-doubt flushed cheeks, Grace's running clothes coupled with a perky ponytail and cherry lip gloss, the determined set of Max's head, and Anarchy's hewn expression. "You're still here?"

It was an unconscionably rude thing to say to a guest in my home. I smiled at her. That raise I'd been thinking about was effective immediately.

Anarchy focused his gaze on me. "I mean it, Ellison. Stay out of this investigation." He turned and stalked out of the kitchen.

"Anarchy, wait."

He paused outside the door. "Brooks Harney worked for Kathleen O'Malley."

The air around him stilled. "How do you know that?"

"She told me at Brooks' funeral."

He shook his head as if he despaired of my intelligence. "Stay. Out."

"I'm not in."

"Hmph." He resumed his stalking, disappearing down the hall.

I jerked my chin at Grace. "Let him out then lock the door."

She rolled her eyes but did as I asked.

When she'd disappeared through the hall door, I collapsed against the counter, took a deep breath and held it. My heart still raced and the ghost of Anarchy's touch still traced my skin. The kitchen was ridiculously warm. I loosened the top button of my blouse and released the breath I was holding.

"He's very high-handed," said Aggie.

"Very." I studied the grain of the hardwood floor.

"He can't stop me—stop us—from asking questions."

"No." I agreed. "He can't."

"How did he know we'd been to see Stormy?"

"She told him."

Max got up, went to his water dish, and drank deeply.

Aggie wagged a finger at him. "Don't you drip water all over my clean floor."

He dripped water on her clean floor.

"Aggie?"

"Yes."

I fanned my face with my hand. "Do you know how to make crab rangoon?"

"Yes."

"Perfect. I have to go to that Halloween party tonight but would you make some? Soon?" If I was going to be around Anarchy, I needed a regular source for crab and cream cheese or I might spontaneously combust.

TEN

I looked at the man waiting on my front stoop and blinked.

Once. Twice. Multiple times.

It was official. Hell had frozen over. Hunter Tafft was wearing a pink suit.

True, he made an incredibly handsome Gatsby. But pink?

He stepped forward and dropped a kiss on my cheek. "You look lovely."

"Thank you," I murmured. "Won't you come in?"

Grace, who was thundering down the front stairs, paused mid-step. "I thought you might be Camille." She tilted her head. "Gatsby and Daisy, right?"

Not by my intention. How was I to know Hunter would come up with a pink suit to go with my flapper costume?

"We'll have a happier ending," said Hunter.

One would hope since Gatsby ended up shot in a pool.

"Speaking of Camille, Aggie bought stovetop popcorn and Orange Crush for you."

Grace rocketed down the rest of the stairs and joined us in the foyer. "Did she get pudding pops?"

"Yes."

"Well, I guess if we're going to have to stay home..."

"You are. You're grounded." Letting Camille spend the night was a huge concession on my part.

"Fine." Grace infused the word with enough teenage angst to tighten my spine, then she headed toward the kitchen before I could think of a suitable response. Not that she'd have listened to a word I said. Not if her ponytail, swishing with the injustice of being grounded, was any indication.

"She's a good kid," said Hunter.

I didn't argue. She was. Most days. "Would you like a drink?" I led him into the living room where a full ice bucket waited next to various bottles. "What'll it be?"

"Scotch and water."

I dropped ice cubes into a cut crystal glass, poured a healthy finger of scotch over them, then added a splash of water. "Did Libba tell you about my costume?" She must have, there was no way a man just decided to wear a pink suit.

"I asked." He coupled his admission with a blinding smile—the kind that traveled from his mouth to his eyes to my stomach where it incited flip-flops.

The problem with Hunter Tafft was that he was too damned good looking. And charming. He was too damned charming as well. I handed him his drink.

"I hope you don't mind that I came as Gatsby."

"Of course not." I minded. Nothing said *serious couple* like matching costumes. I poured some wine in a glass then raised it. "Cheers."

Hunter clinked his scotch against my glass. "To the most beautiful woman I know."

Not true but said with such sincerity that he left me tongue-tied. His toast required thanks but the signals from my brain to my mouth had lost their way. Maybe those signals were flip-flopping with the remains of Hunter's smile somewhere in my intestines. I took a small sip of wine. "Where did you find a pink suit?"

"That's my secret." He sparkled at me—eyes, teeth, tan. "Your dress is stunning."

At least that was true. "Thank you. I found it in a vintage shop in Paris." With my free hand, I smoothed the fabric over my hip. A million Champagne colored bugle beads shimmied with the movement. "Libba's attending the party with Jay. Did she also tell you that?"

Hunter's thousand-watt smile dimmed. "No. She left that part out."

"It's always so crowded. I imagine we can avoid them if we try." It was disloyal of me to even suggest such a thing, but the thought of another evening spent in Jay's numbing company made me tired.

"I like the way you think."

I took a step back, a step away from Hunter's pink-suited perfection. First dressing like a couple, now making a plan for a party. It was too much.

He reached out and caught my wrist, stopping me from moving farther away.

"Ellison." His voice was as smooth and intoxicating as the black label scotch in his glass.

My stomach gave up on flip-flops. It fluttered. Not butterfly flutters. Butterflies suggest the gentle motion of delicate wings. The fluttering in my stomach was more akin to a flag in a gale.

Using his hold on my wrist, Hunter pulled me closer to him. He smelled of some cologne I couldn't identify—something manly and delectable.

He put his scotch down on the drinks cart and took the wine glass from my hand.

I should have objected, but he was a charmer and I was mesmerized.

The distant *brngg brngg* of a telephone should have brought me to my senses. It didn't.

The fact that I'd already been kissed that day should have paralyzed me. It didn't.

That Hunter and I were wandering down a path that could lead to an altar should have stopped me dead in my tracks. It didn't.

Such is the power of Hunter's charm. I wanted him to kiss me—even if he was wearing a pink suit. And who could blame me? The truth was he wore the damned thing better than Redford.

His lips touched mine and fireworks went off around us.

Bursts of light and energy that exactly mirrored the explosions in my veins.

His lips moved.

I melted.

Hunter. Ellison. A simple, dangerous equation.

"Mom." Grace stood at the door. Her eyebrows had disappeared into her hairline and her eyes were as big as the coasters that protected the drink cart's polished cherry finish from the sweat of our glasses.

Hunter released me. Slowly.

"What is it, Grace?" The heat that warmed my cheeks probably left me more pink than Hunter's suit.

"There's a woman named Priscilla Owens on the phone. I told her you were busy." The skin across the top of Grace's nose wrinkled. Apparently Grace did not much approve of what I'd been busy with. "She insists on speaking with you."

"Fine." My tongue held onto the *n*, making me sound surly and unpleasant. I took a breath. "I'll take it in the study. Hunter, would you excuse me a moment please?"

I didn't wait for his answer. I lifted my chin and brushed past my now smirking daughter.

In the study, I turned on a lamp and picked up the phone on my late husband's desk. "Hello."

"Mrs. Russell?"

"What can I do for you, Miss Owens?"

"I was hoping we could meet."

She wanted to meet? "About what?"

"I was hoping you could tell me what you'd learned about Brooks' death."

I was silent. Seconds ticked by.

"Please?" A sound traveled through the phone line, the half-gulped sob of a woman trying not to cry.

"I don't really know anything."

"Apparently I didn't either." This she said with enough sourness to curdle cream. "Please?"

Brooks Harney had been a complex young man. Was it his sister's death that haunted him or his mother's blame? And the women. So many women. Stormy. But also, according to Kathleen O'Malley, multiple women at Club K. And finally, Priscilla, almost old enough to be his mother and fighting tears.

"I don't know what I can tell you."

"Please?" The word was positively ragged with emotion.

How could I refuse her? "Fine. Tomorrow morning for coffee?"

"I usually get home from a night's work around six. Could we meet in the afternoon?"

"Three o'clock? Do you know the little French place on the Plaza? La Bonne Bouchée?"

"I do. I'll be there. Thank you."

"I'll see you then." I replaced the receiver and glanced around Henry's study. I really did need to call a decorator. With lighter fabrics and the removal of the heavy leather club chairs it might become a room I'd actually use. I crossed to the windows and fingered the drapes. Heavy and dark and not my taste. Rather like Henry had been.

"What are you doing?" Grace asked from the door.

"Nothing. Why?"

"You are doing something. You're avoiding Mr. Tafft."

"I most certainly am not." I was. Considering drapes when there was a guest in the living room was terribly rude, but...

"What's with all the kissing?" Grace's pretty face screwed up into a sucking-lemons expression.

"Adults do kiss, Grace."

"Well, duh. But two men in one day?"

"That, young lady, is none of your business."

"Don't you think you should pick one? They both seem to like you. A lot. And—" a devilish grin lit her face "—you seem to like them too."

"Therein lies the rub," I murmured.

"Only English teachers are allowed to quote Shakespeare."

At least all the tuition I was paying meant she recognized

Shakespeare when she heard it. "You can be ungrounded if you tell me which play."

She froze. I could practically see the cogs turning above her head. "*Macbeth.*"

"Nope. *Hamlet.* You're still grounded."

The sucking lemons expression returned to her face. She turned on her heel and flounced off.

I gathered my courage and returned to Hunter. "Shall we finish our drinks and go?"

A skeleton lounged on a bench just outside the doors to the country club's main entrance. A variety of pumpkins and pots of hardy mums kept him company.

With his hand at the small of my back, Hunter and I crossed the threshold and were met by the buzz of conversations, the clink of ice in glasses, and rubber spiders hanging from the ceiling.

We walked down the hall and worked our way into the crowd.

"Drink?" Hunter asked.

"Please. An old fashioned."

"I'll be right back."

He disappeared into the throng near the bar and I nodded to Amy McLiney Hart. She was dressed as a sexy nurse. It's not every woman who can pull off a costume like that, but she did it admirably.

Jane Addison appeared at my side. Jane can smell gossip like Max can smell steak—from a mile away in the driving rain. "I heard you found Brooks Harney."

Not even a *hello*? I did not want to discuss Brooks with Jane. I didn't want to discuss Brooks with anyone. Already I was regretting agreeing to a meeting with Priscilla Owens. "What are you dressed as, Jane?"

Jane wore orange tights and a yellow dress. Feathers sprouted from her head like grass in springtime.

"Big Bird. Is it true? Did you find him?"

Where was Hunter with my drink?

"Yes," I admitted.

Her eyes lit like Roman candles and she leaned toward me. "I'd heard he was in town, but I hadn't seen him."

I blinked. "You heard he was in town?"

"Kathy Dunn—" she jerked her head toward Kathy who was dressed as Cleopatra and stood among a group of women (vipers all) sipping wine "—saw Brooks and Robbie arguing weeks ago."

"Really?" That was actually interesting. "Where?"

"Her cleaning lady missed her bus so Kathy took her home. She said she saw them in midtown."

I'd gotten the impression the Harneys didn't know Brooks had returned home. "And she's sure it was Brooks and Robbie?"

"Positive." Jane took a sip of something nearly as orange as her tights. A tequila sunrise?

"You're here with Hunter?" Her gaze darted to the man in the pink suit walking toward us.

"I am."

"Well, you look fabulous together. Remember if either of you needs to sell a house..." Apparently Jane had made the leap from club party to marriage to combining households.

"The listing is yours. I promise." Any easy promise. I wasn't ready to proceed past club party and wouldn't be anytime soon. Maybe never.

Hunter put a drink in my hand and I took a grateful sip. "Nice to see you, Jane," he said. "You make a gorgeous Big Bird."

Of course he figured out her costume in seconds flat. How did he even know who Big Bird was?

Jane pushed her shoulders back, stretched her neck, and—God's truth—wriggled her tail feathers. "Thank you. You and Ellison are wonderful as Gatsby and Daisy. You're sure to win the couples' costume contest." She shifted her gaze to someone over my shoulder. "Is that Linda Edenfield Gadegaard?"

I glanced behind me. It was in fact Linda and she was dressed as Alice in Wonderland.

"Excuse me." Jane was already walking away. "I hear she's thinking of selling her house."

I looked up at Hunter. "Jane just told me something interesting."

"I would expect nothing less." His voice was a dry as one of Daddy's martinis.

"She says Robbie and Brooks were seen arguing."

"Oh?"

That was it? Oh? Perhaps my dislike of Robbie Harney colored my judgment, but he had more than a million reasons to kill his brother. How easy would it have been for him to follow Brooks to work? He could easily have rented a clown suit...

The clown suit! Was Anarchy calling the costume rental companies to see if a clown suit hadn't been returned?

"You've got that look."

"What look?"

"The one you get before you land yourself in the hospital. What are you thinking?"

"That the killer might have rented his costume."

"And you want to call the rental companies?"

I did. The clown had scared me half to death and murdered Brooks. I wanted him caught.

"If I were you—" Hunter reached out and tucked a strand of hair behind my ear "—I'd have Aggie call. She's good at this sort of thing."

There. Right there. That was the reason I didn't end things with Hunter. He didn't tell me to be careful. He didn't tell me to let the police handle it. He gave me solid advice and trusted that I'd act responsibly. No other man, not my father, not Anarchy Jones, not even Mr. Coffee, had that kind of faith in me. I raised up on my tiptoes and kissed his cheek. "Hunter?"

He caught my free hand and held it. He even stared into my eyes. "What?"

"Why did Brooks have your card?"

"That's your question?" He shook his head as if I'd

disappointed him. "I honestly don't know. He never contacted me. The only thing I can think of is that he might have wanted a copy of his grandfather's trust. My father drafted it when Brooks was born."

Hunter sometimes bends rules, he might even skirt rules, but he doesn't actually break them. I was pretty sure the contents of someone else's legal documents were privileged. If I asked directly about the terms of the trust, he wouldn't tell me. "I suppose it's the usual. The corpus divided equally among the siblings."

He took a sip of his drink and nodded. His eyes sparkled as if he knew what I was doing and was amused.

"So," I continued, "With Brooks dead, both Robbie and Camille will come into a larger share."

He gave my hand a squeeze. "I can't comment."

He didn't have to. I knew the answer.

"What about—"

Libba appeared next to us and kissed the air next to my cheek. "Great dress."

Bob Mackey had nothing on Libba's costume designer. Cher could only hope to look as glitzy and slinky and toned as Libba did.

"That's quite a costume," I said. Hunter said nothing; he couldn't comment and still remain a gentleman.

"Lighten up, Daisy," said Libba. "It's Halloween, the one time of year I can get away with dressing like this."

"Are you saying you want to dress like that all the time?" The glitter and the rhinestones and the sequins?

She rolled her eyes. My best friend and my daughter had a lot in common when it came to their expertise in rolling their eyes toward heaven. Libba tugged at the edge of her neckline covering maybe an extra quarter inch of her breast. "What do you think, Hunter?"

Hunter allowed his gaze to rest on Libba for less than a second. "Very fetching."

"Fetching?" she asked.

"Fetching." If one says *fetching* often enough, it sounds ridiculous. At least it did when Hunter said it.

Libba narrowed her eyes. "You and Ellison really are a perfect match."

Hunter inclined his chin and his grip on my hand tightened. "Thank you."

"I didn't mean that as a compliment."

Hunter grinned. "I know."

"Hold on to him, Ellison. Not every man has a sense of humor."

As if on cue, a man without a sense of humor joined us. Jay Fitzhugh kissed my cheek. "Ellison, you look lovely."

I murmured my thanks.

"Tafft, nice suit. You wear it well, old sport." Jay, who was dressed as a doctor, draped his arm around Libba's shoulders. "It's been a while since I read Gatsby, but wasn't he some sort of Johnny-come-lately?"

"He transformed himself to get the woman of his dreams," I said.

"Right, right," said Jay. "Everything was about Daisy. If I remember correctly, Gatsby was a salesman."

I held up my bourbon-filled glass and shook it until the ice clinked against the sides. "He was a bootlegger."

"Gatsby was a criminal." Somehow Anarchy Jones had snuck up on us. "Tafft, I need to ask you to come down to the station."

"What?" My voice might—might—have been a *bit* shrill. Or incredibly shrill. What was Anarchy thinking? There was no way in the world Hunter had anything to do with Brooks' death.

"We've been going through Harney's apartment and we have some questions for Mr. Tafft." Anarchy wore his cop face. Hard, unyielding, deadly serious.

"Am I under arrest?" Hunter rubbed his chin and raised a brow as if he found the situation amusing.

Anarchy considered the question. "No. Not yet."

"This is ridiculous." I glared at Anarchy.

He merely crossed his arms over his chest and waited.

"I mean it. You can't possibly suspect Hunter of murder."

Around us people were starting to stare. Especially Jane, whose nose was twitching at the smell of fresh, juicy gossip. I took a deep breath and sealed my lips.

"If Mr. Tafft is innocent, he has nothing to worry about." Anarchy was using his cop voice, as cold and unyielding as his face.

Jay guffawed. Some help he was.

"Mr. Tafft had nothing to do with Brooks' death."

Neither man paid the slightest attention to me. They were caught in some kind of staring match. Hunter in his pink suit versus Anarchy in an ugly plaid jacket. Lawyer versus cop. Bend the rules versus color in the lines.

Was this even about Brooks Harney?

Of course it was. It had to be.

Anarchy didn't break rules. He wouldn't use his badge to harass my date. Then again, if he wanted to question Hunter there were plenty of opportunities besides the club party to request that he come to the station.

Hunter reached inside his pink suit and withdrew his wallet. From that, he withdrew a business card. "Call Nick." He held the card out to me. "You'll get his answering service. Tell them it's duck club business. They'll put you through. Have him meet me at the station."

I took the card from his fingers. Nick Carruthers, attorney-at-law. Why did Hunter need an attorney?

"Oh." Hunter thrust his hand into his pocket and pulled out his keys. "You'll have to drive yourself home."

I took the keys and glared at Anarchy Jones. He could easily have called Hunter and asked him to come down to the station instead of...instead of accosting him during the club party.

Granted, Hunter seemed more amused than annoyed or worried.

"Call Nick." Hunter leaned toward me, caught the nape of my neck with the palm of his hand, and kissed my lips. A kiss that lingered.

Somewhere in the crowd of onlookers a woman tittered.

Hunter pulled away, stroked my cheek with the back of his hand, and said, loud enough for Jane Addison to hear, "I'll miss you tonight."

My jaw dropped. Everyone would think...

I snapped the hinges closed.

Hunter wore a smug expression—entirely different from the urbane one that usually settled on his face like a sophisticated mask.

Anarchy scowled deeply. At Hunter and at me.

I recovered and scowled too. Deeply. That touch, those words, had nothing to do with me and everything to do with one-upping Anarchy.

Then the two of them walked out, leaving me speechless, dateless, and in need of a telephone.

ELEVEN

I did as Hunter asked. I called Nick Carruthers' answering service. I gave the voice on the other end of the line the magic password, my name, and the club's phone number, then waited for a call back.

It took effort not to drum my fingers against the half-wall that separated me from the receptionist. She wore a light blue blouse with a bow tied at her neck and a frown. Guests at parties weren't supposed to hover near her desk.

She looked at me over the top of her glasses, shifted in her chair, then arranged some pencils in a leather cup. "If you'd like to wait in one of the booths, I'll put your call through as soon as it comes in."

"I believe I'll wait here." There was nothing to look at but oak walls in the club's phone booths. I'd go mad. Although, I'd be able to drum my fingers in peace.

The phone rang—well, a red button flashed.

The receptionist snatched the receiver from the cradle, pushed the button, announced the name of the club, then listened. "Yes, Mr. Carruthers, I'll put you through right away." She directed her gaze at me. "First booth, line one."

I hurried to the phone booth and pushed the flashing button. "Mr. Carruthers?"

"Mrs. Russell? What's happened?" His voice was clipped. All business.

"Hunter Tafft has been taken to the police station for questioning. He wants you to meet him there."

"Questioning? Questioning about what?"

"Brooks Harney's murder."

The silence on Nick Carruthers' end of the line was a tangible thing, as solid as the oak that surrounded me. Finally, he asked, "Which station?"

"Um...the one in the bad part of town."

"None of them are located in nice neighborhoods, Mrs. Russell."

"Downtown. I think. Is there someone you can call? The detective's name is Anarchy Jones."

"Anarchy?"

I nodded, remembered he couldn't see me, and stopped. "Yes."

"This just gets better and better."

"You know him?"

"I've got to go." On that less than reassuring note, my lawyer's lawyer hung up on me.

I stared at the receiver in my hand. What to do? I cracked the door and scanned the hallway. Empty.

Without so much as a backward glance, I tiptoed down the hallway away from the party. It wasn't as if I could go have another cocktail. Not when my date had been led away by a police detective.

My plan was simple. Go home. Change out of my flapper frock. Drive to the police station. Convince Anarchy to release Hunter. What could go wrong?

I drove home in Hunter's enormous Mercedes, only half aware of street signs and stoplights. The night pressed against the car's windows. My thoughts pressed back.

It was impossible—totally impossible—that Hunter was involved in Brooks' murder.

But the bloodied business card. Why had Brooks had it?

What did Anarchy know? Why had he felt the need to take Hunter in for questioning during a party? Did he want to embarrass Hunter in front of his peers? Or was there a legitimate reason?

My stomach moved in a queasy side-to-side motion and my temples throbbed. I pulled into the drive, parked, got out of the car, locked the door, and took four fateful steps toward the front door.

"Stop there." The voice came from the darkness

I peered into the shadows cast by the bushes that flanked my front stoop. A better plan might have been to run for the door. That or get back into Hunter's tank of a car and lock the doors. Hindsight. Twenty-twenty.

Stormy's brother, the one with the weak chin and sagging jacket, emerged from the darkness.

Thank God he wasn't a knife-wielding clown. "What do you want?" Relief colored my voice.

"I want our money." The glow from the sconces that flanked the front door cast just enough light to reveal the size of his pupils. They were enormous.

A breeze stirred the dried leaves on the yard, carrying the scent of autumn and cheap whiskey.

I shook my head. "I have no control over Brooks' inheritance. I can't help you."

"Maybe not, but you know who can." He reached behind his back and pulled out a knife. "You tell me who or I'll cut you."

A knife? Seriously? Maybe I should have been frightened but since June I'd been shot at, nearly poisoned, had my house set fire, and almost drowned. A simple knife didn't strike fear in my heart.

I glanced down at my delicate high-heeled shoes. Could I run fast enough to get inside before he caught me? Doubtful. I fingered Hunter's keys, searching for the one that would fit the car door. "Look, Mr...." I didn't know his name.

"Mack. Earl Mack."

Perfect. Mr. Mack with the knife. "Mr. Mack, I have no control over those trusts. Your best course of action is to consult an attorney."

Mr. Mack with the knife showed his opinion of lawyers by spitting on my driveway.

Ugh.

"I'm sorry. I can't help you."

"When I'm done cutting you, I'll go inside and cut Harney's sister, then I'll cut your pretty daughter. I've been watching them through the window." He licked his lips then laughed as if he'd said something funny.

He'd been spying on Grace. Threatened Grace. My blood ran cold. Then hot. "You stay away from my daughter."

"We want what's ours." He waved the knife at me. It glinted in the sconces' light.

I should have been terrified. Maybe if he'd been dressed as a clown I would have been. I was too angry, my blood still boiling over his threats against Grace, to be scared. "I can't help you."

He stepped closer to me and the scent of cigarettes and rotgut liquor tried to swallow me.

I stepped back, staring at the knife. Was it the same one that killed Brooks? Another step. My heel caught. I tripped and fell backward. I twisted and my hip rather than my head hit the pavement. The impact jolted through me. I closed my eyes for a second.

When I opened them, Earl loomed over me, glaring with pupils the size of quarters. There was more going on with him than too much whiskey. He was on something. There was no way his pupils could be so large without a little help from cocaine or some other drug. He sniffed, wiped his nose with the back of his hand, and smiled. Dentistry. Why do people overlook the importance of regular trips to the dentist?

I was willing to bet the value of the Harneys' trust that his smile was meant to intimidate me. It didn't. I was too busy counting rotting teeth. Besides, Earl needed a chin to achieve intimidating.

Still, the Earl leaning over me seemed an altogether different man than the sad sack who'd trailed after Stormy on her way to the family pew at Brooks' funeral. He was almost sinister, possibly dangerous.

Lights swept the lawn and the quiet purr of an expensive engine preceded an automobile coming up the drive.

The headlights caught Earl in their glare. He froze like a deer. Then, unlike a deer, he unfroze. Unfroze and ran.

My father leapt out of the car and looked at me. "Are you all right?"

"Fine," I lied.

Daddy stared at me for a moment then sprinted across the lawn. Had he lost his mind? What did a sixty-year-old man hope to accomplish against an armed man half his age who was emboldened by coke?

My mother was slower to get out of the car. "Ellison." Her voice cut through the night, sharper than Earl's knife ever hoped of being.

"I'm here." I pushed myself up on my elbows. The throb in my hip told me I wouldn't be getting off the ground without help. "Where's Dad?"

"Gone." Mother yelled into the night, "Harrington."

My father didn't answer. My heart skittered in my chest. Had something happened to him? Had Mr. Mack with the knife hurt him?

"Who was that?" Mother demanded.

"Brooks Harney's brother-in-law."

"What was he doing here?"

"Threatening me." The real question was what had happened to my father.

"Jane called us from the club. What did you do to get Hunter hauled away?"

"Nothing," I snapped.

"Well." Her disapproval of my tone—of me—was made evident by the set of her shoulders and the audible exhalation of her offended breath. She turned her head away from me. "There's your father now."

My father, one hand plastered against his right side, stumbled up the drive. "He got away." Daddy bent over and rested his hands on his knees. His chest heaved.

"He had a knife, Harrington. What were you thinking?" Mother used the scandalized tone she usually reserved for my sister and me.

Daddy ignored Mother's question and stared at me. "Why are you still on the ground?"

"I hurt my hip."

He leaned down and offered me a hand.

I put my fingers inside his and he pulled me to standing.

"What the hell is going on?" Daddy's white hair stood out from his head and even in the half-light his cheeks looked ruddy. Anger or exertion? Maybe both. "Who was that?"

I swallowed and smoothed the crushed beads on my dress. "Brooks Harney's brother-in-law. His name is Earl Mack. He thought I could get his sister access to Brooks' trust fund."

"Why would he think that?" My father crossed his arms and glowered at me.

"Um..."

"Why, Ellison?"

I glanced at Mother. The trip to Stormy's had been her idea. Sort of. She hadn't planned on *my* going. Nothing good would come of telling my parents I'd driven Aggie. Not when Mother was furious with me. Not when Daddy's lips were stretched back from his clenched teeth.

"I'm not sure."

I scratched my nose. It itched too much not to.

"You're lying." Daddy growled the words.

I didn't argue.

He shook his pointer finger at me. "I am tired of worrying about what disaster is going to befall you next. I almost had a heart attack when we pulled up the drive and saw a man with a knife."

"Now, Harrington, it's not as if Ellison invited that horrible man to attack her."

"Ellison involves herself in situations that lead to trouble." The look on his face dared us to argue. His furious gaze settled on me. "Now, why would he think you could get him access to the Harney money?"

Because I'd gone to his house with Aggie and talked about trusts as if I understood them.

"Maybe he found out Aggie works for her." Mother spoke in a hushed tone.

"What has Aggie got to do with this?" My father's voice warned of a storm gathering on the horizon.

"Aggie used to be a private detective." Mother shifted her weight from her left foot to her right. Lines puckered her forehead. She was nervous. Daddy doesn't get mad often, but when he does—watch out.

"So?" Daddy was never short with Mother. God help us when this storm broke.

"I suggested—at the Harneys' request—that Aggie verify that woman was really Brooks' wife."

"So Aggie butted in and now a man with a knife has threatened Ellison." My father's face filled with thunder and lightning. "This is your fault."

Mother's response was a sharp intake of breath. Her eyes narrowed. Her shoulders squared. Boadicea stood ready for battle in my driveway.

Oh dear.

The last time Mother and Daddy fought, the toxic cloud of affronted feelings hung around for weeks. Weeks when Mother insisted on meeting me for coffee. Weeks when Daddy spent days on the golf course and nights nursing arid martinis. Weeks that felt like years.

All things considered, I preferred having Mother and Daddy mad at me as opposed to each other. "It's not Mother's fault. It's mine."

They left off scowling at each other and turned their choleric gazes on me.

"Oh?" One word from Mother and I was sixteen and late for curfew. Of course, that one word was spoken with the absolute certainty that Frances Walford was never wrong.

"I went to Stormy's house with Aggie. I didn't want her driving to that neighborhood in her car. It's not reliable. And then I didn't want to wait outside alone."

Mother shook her head. Slowly. She'd given birth to a dimwitted daughter. Then she pinched the bridge of her nose as if my ill-considered actions had given her a splitting headache. Mother's exasperated expression was nothing when compared to the look on my father's face.

Daddy's head lifted from his shoulders and completed a turn. Steam exploded from his ears. "Have you lost your damned mind?"

He didn't expect an answer. His diatribes always began with rhetorical questions.

I answered anyway. "I have not. I can take care of myself." This might have been slightly more convincing if they hadn't arrived to see me on the ground at the apparent mercy of a deranged man with a knife.

"Your mother is right. You need to marry Hunter Tafft."

I'd never been much good with non sequiturs. How had he gone from anger at my visiting a possible criminal and Earl's subsequent visit to my shrubbery to the altar? "Pardon me?"

Daddy's face was as red as the bricks on my house. He raked his finger through his hair and shook his head. "You obviously don't have the sense required to take care of yourself. You're a danger to yourself and others. You need a man to manage you."

Manage me? I recoiled as if he'd slapped me. I even raised my hand to my cheek. Some tiny part of my brain recognized that seeing Earl above me with a knife had frightened my father. Badly. Some tiny part knew his anger was based on love. A tiny, miniscule, microscopic part. A part too small to pay any mind. The large part of my brain curled into a fetal position and wailed.

Mother was supposed to say the cruel things. Not Daddy. Mother considered it her duty to point out my faults and failings. Hem too short. Hair too long. How many drinks does that make? She considered such comments helpful.

Right now she paled and laid a hand on my father's arm as if she sensed he'd gone too far—as if her touch could somehow take back his words.

Children might chant about sticks and stones and words that

could never hurt them, but the truth was words could wound. Deep as knives. My father considered me an incompetent ninny. He thought I needed a man to take care of me, to—his words—*manage* me.

"Thank you for coming to my rescue." I walked toward the front door.

"Where the hell do you think you're going?" He spoke loud enough for his voice to bounce off the walls of my house and echo down the block.

"Harrington, the neighbors."

"I don't give a damn about the neighbors."

Mother did. The thought that my witchy next-door neighbor, Margaret Hamilton, might have been listening to our family argue in the front yard would keep Mother up all night.

All things considered, I sided with Daddy on the neighbor debate. Especially when it came to Margaret Hamilton. Not that I'd admit it tonight. I reached the front door and inserted my key. "I'm going to bed. Good night."

"We're not done." My father's voice boomed.

Mother winced. "Harrington."

"We are done." My words sounded wobbly, unsure. Since I was old enough to toddle, I'd been taught to defer to my father—to men. Standing up to my father flew in the face of nearly forty years of putting a man's wants and needs before my own. What had all that putting a man's needs first got me? A cheating husband and a whole lot of unhappiness. "What I did was no less foolish than chasing after a man with a knife." I straightened my spine. "Being my father doesn't give you the right to say anything you want. I'm not your little girl anymore, Da—" Now was not the time to call my father *Daddy*. I opened the door and slipped inside, closed the door, and turned the lock.

My father pounded his fist on the other side.

I rested my forehead against the door's solid expanse and slid the chain in place.

The sound of my father's fist beating on my door echoed

through the foyer, attracting a curious Max. He cocked his head to the side and growled.

I turned and walked away.

TWELVE

I painted. Daubing color on canvas calmed me. Creating form and structure gave me the illusion of control. The meeting of brush and canvas and paint and inspiration was therapeutic. I needed therapy.

An hour passed.

Then another.

Then the darkness outside the windows lightened until an orange-sherbet tinged shade of lavender caressed the glass. Max lifted his head from his paws, yawned, stretched like a cat, then went and sat by the door.

I washed off my brushes and dropped them into a mason jar to dry. "I suppose you want to go out?"

His stubby tail wagged.

"Fine." I opened the door and he sidled through.

Together we descended the stairs and entered the kitchen. I unlocked and opened the back door then cracked the storm. A rush of cool air swirled around me. The breeze carried the scent of falling leaves.

Max surveyed his domain. Was the squirrel far enough from the oak tree to make the chase worthwhile? Apparently not. My dog ambled outside rather than raced. I leaned against the doorframe and watched him sniff—presumably with his enormous nose he could smell more than leaves.

In the kitchen, Mr. Coffee offered me a flirty good morning. "I've got coffee." He added a wink and a cheeky yellow gingham smile. "All you have to do is push my button."

Sleep or coffee?

My eyes were gritty and my back ached from a night spent standing in front of my easel instead of snuggling in my bed. Fuzz grew in my brain like moss. I needed sleep. "Later," I promised.

"Who are you talking to?" Grace stood barefoot and sneaky quiet next to the backstairs. She'd crossed her arms and tilted her head as if she was deeply worried.

Unfortunately, Max was still outside. I couldn't say I was talking to him. "Mr. Coffee."

She covered her eyes with her palm and shook her head. "Mom, you need a boyfriend."

Exactly what my father had said. Well, except for the fact my father had meant a husband not a boyfriend. And he hadn't been nearly as nice about it.

I snorted. "If you ask me, Mr. Coffee is just about perfect. He's always here when I need him."

"So is Mr. Tafft."

"Mr. Coffee makes no demands and he doesn't tell me what to do."

"Has Mr. Tafft done either of those things? Has Detective Jones?"

"Drop it, Grace."

One of her eyebrows rose in a fair approximation of Mother's Ellison-you're-being-ridiculous expression. "Just pick one so you can stop talking to the appliances."

Pick one? Max's scratch on the storm door saved me from coming up with a witty retort.

I let him in and he marched over to his food bowl and whapped it with one of his paws.

I bent and picked it up. My back creaked and I hid a yawn with my hand.

"Is Camille still asleep?"

"Yep. We stayed up late talking."

"What are you doing up?"

Grace shrugged. "I couldn't stop thinking about what Camille said. She's sad about her brother, but she's sadder that she's the only one in her family who seems to care that he died."

Poor girl. With Max's careful supervision, I scooped two cups of kibble into his bowl and put it on the floor. "Is there anything we can do for her?"

Grace shook her head. "She wants to hang out here for a while. Is that okay?"

"Of course."

Max, totally unconcerned with teenage drama, grinned at me then dug in.

I rubbed my eyes. "Can you handle breakfast? I was up all night and I'm going to lie down."

"You? Up all night? No wonder you're talking to the coffeemaker. What happened?"

I yawned. "I'll tell you about it when I wake up."

"You had a fight with your mother?"

Close but no cigar. "Not exactly. We'll talk later." I was simply too tired to tell her about last night.

I trudged up the stairs and collapsed into bed.

Four hours later, I awoke with the sense I should be doing something important—something along the lines of following Hunter Tafft to the police station in his car so he had a ride home when Anarchy finished with his questions.

Sweet nine-pound baby Jesus.

I sat up so fast stars shimmered around my head.

I leapt out of bed but my feet slowed before I hit the bathroom. Why was I running? Hunter was probably long since home. I didn't owe him a ride; I owed him an abject apology. I dropped my head to my hands and almost walked into the bathroom door.

"Damn."

I'd never groveled in my life but today was the day.

I yanked a washcloth from the towel rack, wet it, scrubbed last night's mascara off my eyes, then glanced in the mirror. I still looked like a deranged raccoon.

I sighed, turned on the tap in the shower, and stepped in.

The hot water did nothing to wash away my guilt. How could I have left him there? Shame swirled in my stomach like the water circling the drain.

With jets of steaming water beating against me, I composed an epic apology speech, then I rinsed, turned off the taps, and toweled dry.

Again I glanced at the mirror. The dark circles under my eyes hadn't budged. They weren't the remnants of generously applied mascara. They were proof I needed more sleep.

I stepped into the bedroom and squinted at the clock. Almost noon. No sleep for me. I had an apology to make before I met with Priscilla Owens at three.

Ten minutes later, I descended the stairs ready to yield to Mr. Coffee's charms. I anticipated yellow gingham and the nectar of the gods. I got Hunter Tafft sitting at the kitchen counter.

At least there was coffee.

I poured myself a cup then turned and faced him. "Would you like a cup?" The carefully worded apology I'd crafted in the shower had flitted away. Disappeared. Left me tongue-tied.

"No, thank you. I came to get my car. Grace let me in." Hunter's perfect shine seemed dimmer, as if a night with Anarchy had somehow tarnished him, as if my failure to appear had wounded him.

"About that—"

He held up his hand as if he didn't care to hear my apology. "I didn't ask you to follow me."

He hadn't asked me to come, but he'd expected that I would. A glimmer of hurt shone in his eyes.

"I was going to follow you to the station, but when I came home to change Earl was hiding in the bushes and he threatened me with a knife—"

"Stop." He held up his right hand. "Who is Earl?"

"Earl Mack. Stormy's brother. He seemed to think I could access Brooks' trust."

Hunter rubbed his left hand across his forehead.

"Good Lord, Ellison. Are you all right? What happened?"

"My parents pulled up and he ran away."

"Did you call the police?"

I glanced at the floor. "Not exactly."

"What *exactly* did you do?" He used his lawyer voice, the sonorous one that could convince a jury of grandmothers the tattoo-covered street thug who'd knocked down their friend, stolen her purse, and been caught red-handed was innocent. It was a voice that demanded an answer.

"I had an argument with my father. We haven't had a disagreement since I was a teenager and—"

"Have you reported that Earl assaulted you?"

"No. Not yet."

He stood, lifted the phone off the hook, and held it out to me. "Call."

My spine stiffened and my heels dug into the floor. "Don't tell me what to do." I sounded like a petulant five-year-old, but I'd had it up to my eyeballs with men expecting me to do what they said just because they said it.

"Call."

"I will." On my own time and not because he'd told me to. I ignored the phone in his hand. "Later."

Ding dong.

"I'll get it." Grace's voice carried down the stairs and interrupted the deep scowl Hunter was sending my way.

I turned to Mr. Coffee—the one man who never tried to manage my life—and refilled my cup. Without offering a single opinion or directive, he provided me with the fuel to face Hunter. I sipped, sighed, took the receiver from Hunter's hand, and, with a flourish, dropped it back on the cradle.

Hunter crossed his arms and shook his head as if I'd disappointed him. Again.

My father strode into the kitchen and the temperature dropped twenty degrees. Obviously he was still in high dudgeon.

Grace followed him in, took the room's measure, grimaced,

and turned on her heel, leaving me to face two angry men alone.

I stood next to Mr. Coffee, my one ally. Well, except for Max. He sat at my feet and regarded with doggy distrust the two men he'd heretofore considered friends.

My father opened his mouth then closed it. Whatever dressing down he had planned for me was stymied by Hunter's presence. Daddy could hardly point out that I was an idiot in front of the man he wanted me to marry.

A small blessing. Tiny. Miniscule.

"Good afternoon."

My father grunted.

"Coffee?"

Another grunt.

"What about you, Hunter? Are you sure you don't want coffee?"

"No, thank you."

They stood in silence. And in this case, silence definitely wasn't golden. It was as prickly and uncomfortable as a hair shirt. I sipped my coffee and pretended to be sanguine. I wasn't. I wasn't raised to displease the men in my life and their mute ire had my insides squirming like a bucket of worms.

Brnng brnng.

I lunged for the phone, sloshing my coffee over the rim of my cup and onto the floor. What a waste. At least I could count on Mr. Coffee to make me more. "Hello."

"Ellison?"

Oh dear Lord. I had nothing to say to the man who'd escorted my date out of the club party. I let silence speak for me.

"Are you there?" he asked. "You're angry."

"You *are* a detective." Sometimes sarcasm is called for. "We both know Hunter didn't kill Brooks." Or Charles Dix—but I wasn't about to bring him up.

Hunter and my father regarded me with interest.

"I had questions."

"They couldn't wait?"

Now it was Anarchy's turn to be silent.

"When I got home—alone, I might add—Earl Mack was hiding in my bushes. He attacked me."

Something on the other end of the phone crashed—the front legs of a chair slamming back to the floor, a coffee mug meeting an untimely end, a load of guilt falling on Anarchy's broad shoulders?

"You're all right?"

"Fine."

"You didn't call it in?"

"I had other things to think about." I scowled at my father.

"We'll need your statement."

"Fine."

"We'll put an extra patrol on your street until he's caught."

"Fine."

"Can you come down to the station?"

His voice tiptoed around my bad mood as if he was afraid the wrong combination of words—the wrong tone—might set me off. If he only knew.

I squinted at the two men standing in my kitchen. "I'm on my way."

It didn't take long to file a police report. I sat in a dingy interview room and explained what had happened, confirmed that when Earl Mack was caught I did want to press charges, and shared my parents' names as corroborating witnesses. Brief. Dry. Emotionless.

"My parents' phone number is three-six-one—"

"Ellison."

I ignored Anarchy's interruption.

"Zero-eight-nine—"

"Ellison, we have your parents' phone number."

"Oh. Well, then." I stood and glanced at my watch. "If there will be nothing further, I'm meeting someone for coffee." Almost two hours remained until I was due to meet Priscilla, but Anarchy did not need to know that. I turned toward the door of the sad little room where I'd recounted my tale. Surely the city budget could stretch for fresh paint and chairs that didn't creak when one moved?

"Wait. Please."

I paused.

"About last night..." His voice trailed away.

I glanced over my shoulder. Gravity seemed to be exerting extra pull on Anarchy. His mouth drooped. The skin around his eyes drooped. Even his shoulders drooped.

"You're right. I shouldn't have picked up Tafft at the club." He pulled at the collar of his denim shirt—apparently he came to work in casual clothes on Saturdays. "I was jealous."

People getting tetanus shots with ten-inch needles wore happier expressions than the one on Anarchy's face. Telling me he'd been jealous had cost him.

"So you broke the rules."

"No." His response was lightning fast. Decisive. "He needed to be questioned."

"But not last night."

"Not last night."

"When Henry died, I swore I was done with men." My late husband had left a sucking wound in my soul, a wound that hadn't yet healed. "But you and Hunter." I bit my lip and searched for words. "I'm not ready. I don't know if I'll ever be ready. You should move on. Both of you." With that, I made my escape.

I drove to the Country Club Plaza and parked in Swanson's garage. I needed retail therapy in the worst way.

An hour later, I stashed three pairs of slacks, two pairs of shoes, four sweaters, and a new coat in my trunk, locked it, and descended to the sidewalk.

La Bonne Bouchée, where I was meeting Priscilla, was several blocks away and I took my time walking, enjoying the mild afternoon. I paused and admired a coat in Halls' window then glanced at my watch. There was just enough time to pop inside.

I popped.

"The coat in the window," I said to a saleswoman. "How much is it?"

She named a number that made my eyes widen.

"Who's the designer?"

"Bill Blass."

That explained why it cost nearly as much as a new mink. I'd just bought a coat at Swanson's, I didn't need a second one. Strictly speaking, I hadn't *needed* the first one.

I sighed and checked the time. "I have to go, but I'll think about it. Thank you."

At precisely three o'clock, I pushed open the door to the little French bakery and took a deep breath of sugar-and-butter-laden air. Somehow I walked past the siren song of a display case filled with French pastries without stopping. A minor miracle. Instead, I scanned the small dining area.

Priscilla waited for me at a table in the corner. If the large number of crumbs on the table were any indication, she had not made it past the pastries unscathed. She saw me and waved.

I weaved my way through the tables and claimed the seat across from her.

"Thank you for meeting me," she said.

"My pleasure." I scratched my nose.

"I'm afraid I started without you. This is breakfast time for me."

"I'm glad you did. Palmier?"

She nodded. "It was delicious."

A waiter appeared and I ordered café au lait.

Priscilla watched him walk away then shifted in her seat. "What you must think of me."

"Pardon me?"

"Middle-aged woman. Younger man. Mrs. Robinson and Benjamin Braddock."

"In truth, I hadn't given it much thought."

Priscilla's mouth thinned.

Did she really imagine I sat at home passing judgment on her?

There were scads of more interesting things to do—watch television, paint, walk the dog, refill Mr. Coffee.

"I didn't plan for it. It just happened."

Cats are attracted to people who don't like them. Put a cat-hater in a room with a tabby and that darned cat's guaranteed to rub up against their shins or jump on their lap, ignoring cat-lovers hither and yon.

That's how it is with me and personal revelations. There are people who like listening to others' problems. Shrinks. Psychologists. Counselors. Me, I'd rather face murderous clowns. Yet everyone I met seemed bound and determined to share their innermost thoughts and emotions.

"Brooks and I cared about each other." Her voice caught. Seemingly Priscilla had cared a lot. Fair enough. But why was she telling me? And, if she cared so much, why had she needed to look up his name in a file?

"Was Brooks the clown every night?"

"No. He had several nights off each week. I never could remember which ones they were." She rubbed her eyes, smearing her mascara. "That's why I opened his file."

"What did he do the nights he wasn't working for you?"

Priscilla's lips pinched together and her eyes narrowed. Seconds passed.

"I'm sure I don't know."

Those must have been the nights he worked for Mistress K. There was no getting around it. I was going to have to call her.

What to say to Priscilla? Brooks Harney had possessed the morals of a tomcat. He'd been married, carried on an affair, and made himself available to female members of Club K. He'd also shown the strength to get himself—and keep himself—off drugs. I made one of those soft humming noises in my throat, a sympathetic sound which was incredibly useful when words abandoned me in the face of another's raw emotion.

"I didn't have dreams of the future." She glared at me as if she expected me to argue. "I didn't." Priscilla was lying. She had dreamed of the future. The tears glimmering at the corners of her eyes were a dead giveaway. "We had fun together."

Really, what could be more fun than an affair with a man half your age? Influenza came to mind.

"We agreed it was just for the season."

"The season?"

"Until the haunted houses closed down."

"Did you know Brooks was married?"

She scowled. "He'd filed for divorce."

That was news. "When?"

"I don't know the exact date, but he filed before he left California." She brushed her crumbs to the floor. "Did you see his wife at the funeral?"

I said nothing. *Everyone* had seen Stormy Harney at the funeral. The question had to be rhetorical.

"How could he have married her?" She rubbed the back of her hand across her lips as if wiping away the taint of lips that had touched both Stormy's and hers. "She's nothing but a two-bit floosy. And tacky. You'd have thought Brooks would pick a girl with some taste—some class—and not one who was out for his money." Her mouth, now entirely free of lipstick, twisted into a sucking-lemons sneer.

That darned cat. Priscilla's jealousy was not something I wanted rubbing against my shins. "You knew about his inheritance?"

"It's one of the reasons he came back here. He'd already met with the trust officer. He planned on calling the lawyer. Brooks was going to establish new accounts, separate from his family." She wiped under her eyes. "He was going to go to college and get a degree in social work. He wanted to help other addicts."

Oh good Lord. Brooks was one of those people? One who *wanted* to listen to other people's problems.

Being a social worker was a far cry from the life Genevieve and Robert had probably planned for their son, but even they would have had to admit that such a career was infinitely preferable to

Brooks dying with a needle in his arm. Or a knife in his chest.

"What do the police know about his murder?" Priscilla wiped under her eyes. Her fingers came away dry.

"They don't share their investigation with me."

"Really? I thought you and that detective..." She didn't finish her sentence, daring me to finish it for her.

"No. There's nothing between us. I can only tell you what I saw. Someone dressed in a clown suit stabbed Brooks."

"And you have no idea who it was?" Why was she so interested? Was I too suspicious? She had had a murderer running around her haunted house. In her Gucci boots, I'd be concerned too.

"Absolutely none," I told her.

The waiter arrived with my coffee and I took a grateful sip. "You know what happened next. I found a security guard." The guard hadn't believed me and Brooks' body had gone missing. "He brought me to you."

I closed my eyes and pictured that night. Scary clowns with knives. If the group of teenage girls who'd followed me into the circus room had seen Brooks' murder, they would have squealed in horrified delight then shuffled forward to the next terrifying scene.

They weren't alone. Almost anyone else would have thought the stabbing was part of the experience—another vignette designed to terrify.

But Brooks had stumbled toward me and I knew dead when I saw it. What's more, he'd slipped business cards in my pocket. Why?

Priscilla and the guard had tried to convince me I was imagining things.

If I hadn't called Anarchy, no one would have ever known Brooks had been murdered in the haunted house.

Was that why the body had been moved? To hide where the actual murder took place?

If that was true, did the woman sitting across from me have something to do with his death?

* * *

I stared at the phone. Sure, it looked innocuous, but...

I shifted my gaze. I was surrounded by Henry's prize possessions.

Really, I ought to go upstairs and call from my bedroom. No—the thought of speaking with Kathleen O'Malley was distasteful enough, I didn't want her voice anywhere near the place I lay my head. Here, Henry's study, was the place to make the call.

I snatched up the receiver and dialed.

The phone rang. Once. Twice. Three times.

"Hello." A male voice.

"May I please speak with Miss O'Malley?"

"Who?"

Dammit. "May I please speak with Mistress K?"

"One moment."

I drummed my fingers on the edge of Henry's desk and waited.

"Hello."

"This is Ellison Russell calling." This call to a dominatrix suddenly seemed like an epically bad idea.

"Yes?" Somehow Mistress K infused the one word with amusement.

"You said something at the funeral."

"Oh?" More amusement.

"You asked me to tell Detective Jones that Brooks had—" I gritted my teeth and glared at my husband's Toby mugs "—played with women at your club."

"That." She sounded less amused. "I talked to all of them. None of them had anything to do with Brooks' death."

"How can you be sure?"

I *heard* her smile.

"They all miss him. Badly. It's hard to find a man who'll drop to his knees on command and—"

"Enough!" I believed her. Hearing more would just scar my ears.

"Are you sure? If you come down to the club, I can tell you who I spoke with. We open at nine."

"I'm sure." I borrowed Mother's best arctic voice.

"Your loss."

"So be it. Goodbye." I hung up the phone. Quickly. There was no point in talking to Mistress K further. I believed her. I couldn't see a dominatrix hiring a man to knife Brooks.

THIRTEEN

I lifted the kitchen phone from its cradle and stared at it. All things being equal, I'd rather find another body or listen to Mistress K's litany of shocking sexual acts than call Anarchy.

I dialed his office number anyway.

A woman answered. "Hello."

"This is Ellison Russell calling with a message for Detective Jones. Please tell him that Priscilla Owens told me Brooks Harney had filed for divorce."

She repeated the message back to me then added, "Is that all?"

"Yes. Thank you." I hung up. Anarchy was smart enough to realize Stormy had a strong motive for murder without my pointing it out. But what about Priscilla? Was jealousy a motive for murder?

"I still can't believe he got married and didn't tell us."

Really, I needed to hang a bell on the door to the backstairs. Camille, having silently descended the stairs, stood just inside the kitchen with her eyes wide and her hands clasped.

Apparently Grace had taken me at my word and invited her friend to stay indefinitely.

"According to Stormy, it was a spur of the moment wedding." I smiled. Why was I smiling as if an unplanned wedding excused all? My cheeks relaxed and the smile fled. "They didn't invite anyone."

Camille's expression reminiscent of her mother's usual demeanor—a combination scrunch of the nose and curl of the lip that suggested the sudden introduction of a foul odor. "What was he thinking?"

Marrying Stormy or not inviting his family? "I don't know, dear."

We stared at each other for a moment then Camille said, "Thank you for letting me stay. Things are awful at home right now."

I used the soft sound in my throat. "You're most welcome. Things will get better. I promise"

She stepped into the kitchen. "I doubt it. My father acts like nothing happened. My mother has taken so many Valium I don't even know if she realizes who died. And Robbie says it's just as well Brooks is dead."

Her parents were morons and Robbie was an uncaring idiot. But they were her family. Camille needed them. I made another soft sound. "May I get you anything? A drink? Are you hungry?" Not that I planned on cooking, but Aggie kept us well stocked with snacks and Tupperware containers filled with good things to eat.

"No, thank you." She pulled out a stool, sat at the counter, and held the tips of her fingers under her eyes, half masking her face. "Robbie's the worst. He says Brooks would have run through his inheritance then come back for more."

It was happening again. Cat, cat-hater, and the rub of secrets and emotions that made me squirm.

"There's no way Robbie could know that."

She shrugged—a defeated little gesture. "He says our grandfather never dreamed his money would be used to finance a drug habit."

"Brooks wasn't taking drugs." Camille ought to know Brooks wasn't as awful as Robbie made him out to be. "He was planning on going back to school. He wanted to work with other addicts and help them get clean."

Camille covered her hand with her mouth as if her fingers could muffle the strangled sound in her throat.

Good Lord. I'd made things worse. I should have kept my mouth shut.

She dropped her head to her hands. "Mother says you can't

trust addicts. They'll break your heart." No child should sound so hopeless.

Genevieve should have kept her mouth shut too.

"Brooks was turning his life around," I insisted. Did that make his death harder or easier to bear?

"It doesn't matter. He's dead." Tears welled in her eyes. She wiped them away with the back of her hand. "I can't believe I won't ever talk to him again. He was my brother and I loved him."

"Of course you did."

"We never saw him, but there was always the possibility that we might. That he and my parents would make up, that he'd come home."

Yet another soft soothing noise came from my throat. I was getting good at them.

"I can't believe—" My witchy next-door neighbor probably heard Camille's swallow. It was that loud. "It's just that—" Camille's nose reddened to cherry tomato and the tears that had been threatening streamed down her drawn cheeks. "I miss him."

I draped an arm around her shoulders.

She sobbed.

I rubbed circles on her back and made yet another soft soothing noise.

Camille cried harder.

Note to self—the soft soothing noise never made anything better. Quite the opposite. It invited confidences and tears.

"It's just so awful." Her shoulders shook beneath my hand.

"Of course it is."

She lifted her head slowly and stared at me. Something other than sadness swam in the pools of her eyes. Fear.

Fear? What was she afraid of? "Camille—"

Brnng, brnng.

Dammit.

"One minute, Camille." I held up a single finger to illustrate then picked up the receiver. "Hello."

"Oh good, I got you."

"Good afternoon, Mother."

Camille climbed off her stool, gave me a small, droopy wave, and disappeared up the back steps. What was she afraid of?

"Ellison." Mother's sharp tone seemed to reflect the knowledge that she didn't have my full attention.

"Yes, Mother."

"You need to apologize to your father."

Now she had my full attention.

"For what?"

"He's moping around the house like a man who's been told he can never play golf again."

"I'm sorry to hear that, but what has that got to do with me?"

"You know exactly. He expects your love and respect. He only said those things because he loves you. He worries."

That might be true—probably was true—but it did nothing to remove the sting of *manage*. And wasn't respect a two-way street? "What exactly am I supposed to apologize for?"

"Not listening to him."

"I did listen. I heard him tell me that I need a man to *manage* me."

"You're being ridiculous. He didn't mean manage. He meant monitor. Someone to keep an eye on you so he doesn't have to worry so much. And, you have to admit, it would be no hardship to have Hunter Tafft watching over you."

"I don't want anyone watching over me. It's my life, Mother."

"There's no need to get snitty."

Snitty?

I stretched the phone cord and filled Mr. Coffee with grounds. "What would be so bad about being on my own?" Nothing. That's what.

"You won't be young and pretty forever."

Meaning I'd better catch a man now while I still had my looks and figure. *Catching a man*. It made me sound like a predator hoping to ensnare some unsuspecting fool in my trap. I filled Mr. Coffee with water.

"You've got two men on a string now. Do you know how easily that number could shrink to none?"

I pushed Mr. Coffee's button. "What if it did?"

The question achieved the impossible; it struck Mother dumb.

"I don't need a man to make me happy."

"You say that now..."

Mr. Coffee—God love him—dripped coffee into his pot. "Mother. Enough."

She huffed. A breath of air that traveled through the phone lines and left a layer of frost on the appliances in my kitchen. "You need to apologize."

"Perhaps Daddy should be the one to apologize."

There was no response. I'd rendered Mother mute twice in one conversation. Somewhere in hell, the damned were having a snowball fight. "You've changed." Her acid tone made that change sound as appealing as a triple bogey. Or worse. "I don't know what's happened to you since Henry died."

I wasn't precisely sure what had happened to me either, but I wasn't going back to being the Ellison I had been. "I'm not going to apologize, Mother. Is there anything else?"

I poured myself a cup of coffee while she thought.

And thought.

"It never occurred to me you'd go with Aggie to see that woman. If it had, I wouldn't have asked her."

"So you're all right with sending Aggie into a potentially dangerous situation but not me?"

"That man didn't come looking for Aggie."

I couldn't argue that point.

"Ellison, we want you safe. Just like you want to keep Grace safe."

I wanted Grace to be safe, but I didn't want her to be packed in cotton until she found a man to take care of her. I wanted her to have a life. I wanted a life. On my own terms. "I appreciate the sentiment. I do. But I'm not going to apologize or consign myself to marriage just so I can have a man take care of me."

"Then who will take care of you?"

"I'll take care of myself." With a little help from Mr. Coffee. "Mother, I've got to go. I'll talk to you later. Love you." I hung up the phone before she could object, then took it off the hook. If—when—she called back, the line would ring busy.

Saturday evening passed in a flurry of Archie Bunker, Mary Tyler Moore, Bob Newhart, and Carol Burnett. I sat on the couch, listened to Archie bully Edith, and thought of the coat I hadn't bought, patterned raw silk somewhere between persimmon and coral with a fur collar and cuffs. I had no place to wear it. It was too expensive. I had a Gucci trench due to be picked up from the cleaners. I didn't need another new coat.

Where would I even wear a coat like that? It wouldn't stand up to daily use. Not like the perfectly lovely coat I'd just bought at Swanson's. I could wear the Halls' coat to the opera or the symphony or on dates. Then again, I could wear my mink on all of those occasions. Except the dates. I wasn't accepting dates.

I drifted to sleep during Carol Burnett. Max nudged me awake with a cold, emphatic nose. It was time for him to go out.

He trotted into the backyard, not a care in the world. It might be nice to be a dog—no coveting coats, no complicated relationships, no worries other than keeping the backyard squirrel-free.

Max finished his business and returned to the back door with every expectation of receiving his nightly dog biscuit.

Of course, I gave him one. Then he followed me upstairs and we both went to bed.

I woke the next morning feeling much better about the world. That's not to say animated blue birds were draping my sweater across my shoulders while tweeting a cheery tune—but I did feel better.

I headed to the kitchen for a confab with Mr. Coffee. He waited there for me. Silent. Dependable. Altogether perfect. One push of his button and he delivered.

Grace opened the door from the backstairs. "Hi, Mom."

Camille followed her. "Good morning, Mrs. Russell."

"Mom?"

"Mmmm?" I took my first sip of coffee and sighed.

"Could we go out for breakfast?"

"Sure."

Now Grace sighed. It might have been a sigh of relief. I make one thing for breakfast. Bisquik pancakes. A recipe that's impossible to screw up—well, almost impossible.

"Where do you want to go?"

There's a new place over on the east side," Grace said.

"Oh?"

"My brother says it sounds like the Moosewood Restaurant."

"Moosewood?" I gazed at Camille over the rim of my coffee cup.

"It's a vegan place in Ithaca," she explained. "I went there when I visited my roommate's family. Her father is a professor at Cornell."

"Are you a vegetarian?" I'd ordered the girls pepperoni pizza for dinner and Camille hadn't said a thing.

"No."

That was a relief. "This restaurant, do they at least serve eggs?"

Camille shook her head.

"No eggs?" What was brunch without eggs? "We could always run over to the club."

Grace rolled her eyes. "Come on, Mom. Step outside your comfort zone."

"Fine. Can you be ready in twenty minutes?"

"Fifteen."

Twenty minutes later we were on our way. Grace gave me the address, and I didn't even raise my eyebrows.

The building was purple—a deep violet shade. Bamboo grew out of pots flanking the door. The windows—there were two—had peace symbols painted on them. The sidewalk was cluttered with a mismatched assortment of tables and chairs

"Here?" I asked.

Stepping out of my comfort zone was looking like a gastronomical disaster.

"Here."

I got out of the car. The cool mom, ready for a culinary adventure. "Lock your doors." Hopefully the car would still be here when we finished.

We stepped into a dim restaurant—those peace symbols blocked a lot of light. Trailing ivy in macramé hangers hung from the pressed tin ceilings. The walls were covered with art. Good art by local artists. Perhaps it wouldn't be so bad.

"Three?" asked a hostess with granny glasses and pigtails.

"Yes."

"This way." She led us through the maze of tables.

That's when I saw it.

The coat—the one from Halls' window. The one that had haunted my dreams.

That coat with its luscious fur collar had no business in a restaurant where people didn't eat meat. Then again, it had no business being worn on a Sunday morning.

Either the woman whose shoulders it covered didn't know better, or the man who'd bought it for her was with her and she wanted to please him.

My gaze shifted to Jay Fitzhugh.

He saw me and the color ran from his face like a watercolor left in the rain.

The woman turned and looked at me.

She was definitely not Libba. Not that Libba would be caught dead at a brunch that lacked eggs, bacon—I scanned the room and failed to spot a bar—and Bloody Marys.

"You girls go on and get seated. I see a friend." I strode toward Jay's table.

He stood, knocking his chair over backward. "Ellison."

"Jay. Good morning." I could have insisted that he sit. I didn't. Instead, I gazed down at the woman with whom he was eating breakfast.

Very pretty. Very young.

"I'm Ellison Russell." I extended my hand.

"Alice Steele." She smiled at me and shook.

"Alice is my secretary," said Jay. "We've been working hard, so I thought as a treat—"

"That's a lovely coat, Alice." It draped around her shoulders like a bit of advertising copy. *I am a rich man's mistress.* Or possibly *I'm sleeping with my boss.*

She glanced at Jay then stroked the collar. "Thank you."

"Didn't I see one like it in the window at Halls'?"

"I fell in love with it." She cut her gaze at Jay.

I too looked at Jay. How dare he do this to Libba? She thought he cared for her when in reality he was having some kind of fling with his secretary. "How long have you and Jay—Mr. Fitzhugh—worked together?"

"Since the beginning of the year."

"Well, I'm sure he's very lucky to have you helping him. Do you come here often? I've never been." And I'd never be back.

"It's Jay's favorite." Alice's voice was low and husky and soft as the fur around her neck.

Jay, not Mr. Fitzhugh. And she knew his favorite restaurant. Or thought she did. If I needed any further confirmation of an affair, there it was.

Jay cleared his throat. "This place is a bit off your beaten path, Ellison. What brings you here?" This restaurant was the perfect place to bring someone Jay didn't care to be seen with. It was his bad luck that Grace and Camille had talked me into coming.

"Teenagers." I nodded at the table where the girls were sitting. Grace had her back to me but Camille was regarding Jay with a puzzled expression in her eyes. "I won't keep you from your brunch. Alice, it was so nice to meet you. Jay—" I glared at him "—I imagine I'll see you soon."

I made my way through the maze of tables, claimed my seat and waved at the waiter. I needed coffee.

The young man, who wore a tie-dye t-shirt, a ponytail, and

holey jeans, meandered over. "I'd like a cup of coffee please. Right away."

"You drink a lot of coffee, Mom."

"Mind your own business, Grace."

She wrinkled her nose at me. "May I have some apple juice, please?"

The waiter jotted down her order.

"Who was that you were talking to?" Grace asked.

"Jay Fitzhugh."

"Who?"

"He's a friend of Libba's."

Camille looked up at the waiter. "May I please have a glass of carrot juice with wheat grass?"

Ugh.

"I feel as if I've seen him before." Camille handed over her menu and I hadn't even looked. "May I have the house made granola, please?"

I picked up the menu and scanned.

Dear Lord. Buckwheat groats with bananas and chocolate sauce? What was a groat? A tofu scramble? Butternut squash tacos? At least there were pancakes on the menu. Lord only knew how they made them without eggs or milk.

The pancake recipe was the least of my worries. I put the menu down on the table.

I was going to have to tell Libba I'd seen Jay. I was going to have to tell her about the secretary and the coat. How?

FOURTEEN

I wrapped the phone cord around my finger and pulled until the tip turned as burgundy red as the tufted leather desk chair behind Henry's desk.

Brngg. That made three rings. Where was Libba?

I drummed my fingers on the desk and let my gaze wander. The study really did need a redo. I ought to call a decorator. Choosing between paint and fabric swatches would be far more entertaining than dealing with Libba's cheating boyfriend, my angry parents, a disgruntled lawyer and police detective, and a young man who'd ended up dead.

Brngg.

Maybe I'd replace the carpet.

No.

Definitely I'd replace the carpet. It still held the lingering odor of Henry's cigars. Worse, my late husband had insisted on beige shag.

The floor looked as if it had mange.

Brngg. I'd give it two more rings.

"Hello." Libba sounded breathless, as if she'd run for the phone.

"It's me."

"Jay said you'd be calling."

"Did he?" Dryness infected my voice.

"He said you saw him at brunch with his secretary and that you might have misconstrued things."

Ha! "I didn't misconstrue anything."

"So you don't think he's having an affair with the girl?"

Stick a toe in the water or dive right in? I dove. "He's definitely having an affair with that girl. I'm sure of it."

"Don't sugar coat things for me." Now Libba's voice was dry.

She'd dated cross-dressers, drunks, and married men. One middle-aged cheater was nothing. "You can take it."

"But I don't want to. Not anymore." There was a defeated quality to her voice I didn't like. "Why can't I just find some nice man who wants to take me out to dinner and have sex three times a week?"

I had no answer. Especially not to the second part of her question.

"I don't want a ring or a promise or even a key to his house, just a decent-looking man." It was still there, an un-Libba like sadness I understood all too well. We'd been raised to depend on men, but men were proving to be entirely undependable. "Oh, and I'd like him to have a clean bill of health and not share his willy with every woman he meets."

"His willy?"

"You'd prefer I call it a—"

"Never mind. What exactly did Jay say?"

"He said you seemed mightily suspicious of his entirely innocent relationship with his secretary."

I made a noise in my throat. Not the soft, soothing noise. This sounded more like gagging. "He didn't say that."

"I added the adverbs."

I pinched the bridge of my nose. "Have you seen the coat in the window at Halls'?"

"The glorious one with the fur collar?"

"That's the one. She had it on."

"He didn't give me a coat." The sadness in her voice was now tinged with annoyance.

"You're not twenty-five."

"But I'm me." She paused and I could almost see her rubbing her chin, considering. "Maybe she has independent wealth."

"And maybe I'm Marie of Romania."

"Don't quote Dorothy Parker at me. I don't want to laugh."

"You're better off without him." How many times had those exact words been said about a man? "If ever there was someone unworthy of angst, it's Jay Fitzhugh."

"You're right." She didn't sound convinced. "At least you and Hunter won't have to go on any more double dates."

I didn't comment.

My silence was comment enough.

"You broke up with Hunter Tafft? Have you lost your mind?"

I hadn't. Yet. "You sound like my mother."

That gave her pause. "I don't care. How could you?"

"He didn't appreciate being hauled out of the club party for questioning."

"He can't possibly blame you."

"I forgot to pick him up at the police station."

"You what?" Outrage colored her tone.

"There! You sound exactly like Mother."

"Insulting me isn't going to improve your situation. What are you going to do? He's practically perfect."

Hunter Tafft, practically perfect in every way. It wasn't just Libba's tone that sounded like Mother. My parents approved of him as a glorified governess and Libba approved of him as a—Well, it was best not to think about how Libba would have Hunter take care of me.

"We are not talking about me." My tone was firm.

"I forgot." Libba deadpanned. "It's much more interesting to talk about my problems."

It was. Libba liked sharing and dissecting and emoting.

Not me.

Not. At. All.

"Do you want me to come over?" I'd go if she needed me, armed with a box of tissues, a bottle of wine, and a chocolate cake.

"So I can cry on your shoulder? No." She added a dramatic sigh. "I have symphony tickets."

"You? The symphony?"

"Don't sound so surprised."

"You have a date." There could be no other explanation.

She didn't dispute it.

"No wonder you're not worked up about Jay."

"Oh. I'm worked up. It annoys me immensely that he thought he could lie to me and get away with it."

"What are you going to do?"

"I haven't decided yet." It was all too easy to imagine Libba peering into the gilt mirror that hung above the couch in her sitting room. Perhaps she tried a disdain-filled glare. More likely she checked her teeth for lipstick or wiped a tiny speck of mascara from under her eye. All the while, hatching an evil plot.

"Please, don't TP his house." Libba's ideas of revenge could run to the juvenile.

"Don't be ridiculous, Ellison. He lives on the top floor of a high rise. Besides, I'll think of something much better than that."

Exactly what I was afraid of. Hopefully whoever was taking her to the concert was interesting enough to distract her from doing something legally actionable. "I have a question."

"Yes?"

"Who did Myrtle Kline use when she redid her lake house?"

"Her decorator? Olivia Forde. Why? What are you redecorating?"

"Henry's study."

She mumbled something that sounded suspiciously like *about time,* cleared her throat, then added, "I must dash. I've got makeup repairs to complete before I go."

"Let me know if you need me."

"I will. And Ellison—"

"Yes?"

"Thanks for calling to tell me."

"Anytime." I hung up the phone. Thank heavens Libba hadn't cared much for Jay; I couldn't take one more person being mad at me.

Brngg. Brnng.

I lifted the receiver from the cradle. "Hello."

"Tell me you did not promise your father you'd talk your sister out of that operation." Mother's words were smooshed together by the speed at which she said them.

"I didn't."

"So you have some sense."

I had plenty of sense. "I told Dad I'd talk to Marjorie and tell her how he felt. That's all."

"Have you done that?"

"Not yet. She hasn't called me back."

"He's not very happy with you right now."

An unfamiliar pain pinged inside my heart. I made a habit of disappointing Mother—at least according to her. Disappointing my father was something new. "I'm not very happy with him either."

"You need to fix this."

Me? Why couldn't my father fix the problem? He'd created it. "I'm not apologizing, Mother. Listen, I'm going to go ahead and try Marjorie again. Maybe I can catch her at home. Goodbye."

I pushed down on the hook, released, then dialed Marjorie's number.

Someone answered on the first ring. Not Marjorie. My sister would let a phone ring three times before picking it up even if she was sitting right next to it.

"Hello," said a girl's voice.

"Thea? This is Aunt Ellison. How are you?"

"Fine, thank you. How are you?" Good manners by rote, not interest.

"Fine, dear. May I please speak to your mother?"

"Just a moment, please."

She put the receiver down on a hard surface—the sound echoed in my ear. Seconds later, her distant voice called, "Mom."

Wow. It had taken me years of coaching to break Grace of the habit of bellowing "MOM!" into some poor caller's ear. Sometimes she still forgot.

"She'll pick up in just a minute, Aunt Ellison."

"Thank you. How's school?"

"Fine."

"What are you doing for fun?"

"Nothing much."

"Are you enjoying getting to know David and Aunt Sis?"

"Enjoying?" She sounded puzzled then the manners kicked in. "It's delightful having them here."

Delightful? Thea was a year younger than Grace but she sounded both insincere and world-weary. That or she was bored talking to her aunt.

"Don't you have a birthday coming up?" I asked.

"Next month."

"What did you ask for?"

"They're buying me a car." Not one iota of excitement colored her voice. I'd heard more emotion listening to the time and temperature recording.

"How exciting for you." At least I tried for emotion.

"Yes, very exciting." Her voice was still flat. "Here's Mom."

"Ellison, how are you? I'm so sorry I haven't called you back."

"It's fine. Is everything okay with Thea?"

"Of course. Why do you ask?"

"She just seemed...down." Thea had sounded like she was stealing her mother's Valium.

"Down? Thea? Not at all."

Granted I hadn't seen Thea since Christmas, but the child I remembered was bubbly. A tiny voice in my head whispered *not your problem.* I listened. "Daddy asked me to call."

"Are you going to try and convince me to cancel the surgery?"

"No. Not at all. But Dad is worried for you. He'd prefer that you keep your kidney." He'd also prefer that I get married so my husband could take care of me. My track record with husbands suggested I could do a better job taking care of myself. I gazed up at the coffered ceiling (that could stay—so much more attractive than the carpet). "Daddy loves you."

"I know he does, but his doubting my decision feels as if he's patting me on the head and telling me my opinion is worth less than his just because I'm a woman."

I couldn't argue.

"Things are different now," she said. "He should catch up with the times."

Daddy change? He was more likely to climb Everest.

"I think you're doing the right thing," I said

"Thank you. Your opinion matters." She sounded grateful. Maybe she was. But we both knew the truth. Our father's approval was more important and his disapproval stung.

"You're welcome."

"Elli, I've got a million things to do."

"I won't keep you. Take care of yourself."

"I will. You too."

We hung up and I scanned the study. My parents were mad at me. My sister and I didn't know how to talk to each other. My daughter would be leaving for college in a year or two. I felt very alone and Henry's shag rug was giving me hives. It was definitely time to redecorate.

Aside from calling Olivia Forde and making an appointment for her to come and see Henry's study, I spent the next two days in my studio. Paint plus canvas equaled solace.

I emerged for my standing bridge game—the second and fourth Tuesday of the month. Without fail. I scrubbed the paint off my hands, donned a soft turtleneck sweater, draped a heavy gold chain around my neck, pulled on a pair of gray flannel slacks, and hopped in my Triumph.

The club gardener had planted pansies in the flowerbeds near the drive and their bright faces bent toward the autumn sun. I slowed the car and admired the colors - imperial purple, soft violet, red-winged yellow, and an orange sorbet with a raspberry throat.

I breezed into the clubhouse ten minutes early.

"Good afternoon, Mrs. Russell," said the receptionist.

I stopped at her desk and helped myself to a lemon drop. "Good afternoon. Are we in the green room today?"

"Yes, ma'am."

"Thank you." I strolled down the sun-dappled hallway, humming the song I'd last heard on the radio. "Sunshine on my Shoulders." How apropos.

I took my seat at the bridge table, glanced out the window at an emerald-hued golf course and mums so golden they didn't seem real, and sighed. Today was a better day. I'd worked out my issues in the only way I knew how and the new painting was coming along beautifully.

"You look happy." Libba stood inside the doorway.

"I've been doing some painting. I feel better. How was the symphony?"

"Did you know they don't sing?"

"Why yes, I believe I did."

"Don't be arch. It doesn't suit you." She sank into the chair across from me. "I suppose I knew too. Once. But I'd forgotten."

"What did they play?"

She wrinkled her nose. "Something instrumental."

"They do that."

She covered a yawn with her fingers. "I fell asleep. I don't think my date appreciated it."

"Who was your—"

"Don't." Libba waved her hands. "I do not want to talk about it."

"How about a totally different subject?"

Libba nodded her approval. Thank God. Libba had a better head for minutiae than I. She remembered who dated whom in eighth grade, why they broke up, and who they dated next. She remembered the small slights and the slight acquaintances.

"Do we know Charles Dix?"

"Charles Dix?" She tilted her head to the side.

"That's right."

Libba closed her eyes—a sure sign she was thinking.

I didn't dare interrupt.

With her eyes still closed, she counted on her fingers.

I waited.

"Charles Dix," she murmured. "Didn't Annalise Allen marry a man named Charles Dix? He moved here from—" she wrinkled her nose "—Moline. Or was it Peoria?"

"Where did she find him?"

"They met at college. I think her father got him a job at a bank."

"As a trust officer?"

"That sounds right. Why?"

"He was killed."

Her eyes flew open. "Please tell me you didn't find the body."

Everyone's a comedienne. That Libba, she's a regular Ruth Buzzi.

I had not found his body. I'd found his business card. In the pocket of my coat, put there by a dying clown. "He was killed in a traffic accident." My tone might have been *a bit* arch.

"My, aren't we waspy."

"We most certainly are not."

"Oh please, if you sounded any more like Frances, you'd be her."

And here I thought Libba was my friend. I lifted my nose and stared down its length.

"Why do you want to know about Charles Dix?"

"I found his business card in my coat pocket."

"So?"

"It was the first time I wore the coat."

She arched her left brow.

"His was one of the cards Brooks slipped in my pocket before he died."

"Cards?" Libba rested her elbows on the table and leaned in. "What other cards showed up in that pocket of yours?"

"Am I late?" Daisy rushed into the card room. Per usual, she looked as if she'd dressed in a wind tunnel. Her shirt threatened untucking, her shoes needed a shine, and I'd have bet a hundred dollars the hem of her skirt was being held up with masking tape. She smiled, pure sweetness, and her clothes didn't matter.

"You're right on time," I assured her.

"I beat Jinx?" Daisy scanned the room as if she expected her bridge partner to pop out from under a table. "That never happens."

"Well." Libba sat back in her chair. "I guess even pigs fly sometimes."

Daisy stuck out her tongue and sat. "Very funny."

Jinx appeared in the doorway. "Daisy, you're here." She sounded surprised.

"I'm not always late," said Daisy.

Three sets of brows rose. Mine was one of them.

Jinx joined us at the table. "So, Ellison, I haven't seen you since you found Brooks' body. Tell us about it."

"Don't be such a ghoul," said Daisy.

I picked up a deck of cards from the table and shuffled. "There's not much to tell."

Jinx tilted her head to the side, a curious robin of a woman. "I heard you were at a haunted house."

"Yes."

"What else?"

"Brooks died."

"You're being very insensitive," said Daisy. Thank God for Daisy.

"Oh, please." Jinx waved away Daisy's opinion—and mine—with the flip of her wrist. "It's not as if anyone expected him to live this long. His poor parents have been waiting for a call for years. *I'm sorry, Mr. and Mrs. Harney, your son has overdosed.*"

"He didn't overdose." I returned the cards to the table with slightly too much force. "He was murdered. Shall we draw for dealer?"

"Murder. Overdose. What's the difference?"

"You can't mean that," said Libba.

"Violent death is different." I fanned the deck and pulled the ace of spades. No one else bothered to draw. The high card meant the deal was mine. "It's awful."

Jinx donned a suitably chastised expression and turned her attention on Libba. "I hear you're dating Jay Fitzhugh."

"We went out a couple of times."

"You're done with him already?" asked Daisy.

"Yes." Libba wrinkled her nose. "Why don't you cut the cards for Ellison?"

Daisy cut. "I'm glad to hear that."

"Oh? Why?" Jinx leaned forward.

"That antique dealer I use in Chicago, the one who finds the antique pens, says Jay has been selling antiques. Lots of them."

Jinx and Libba pondered and I dealt (I pondered too). Selling through an out-of-town dealer usually meant trouble. Trouble that needed to be hidden.

"I wondered if perhaps he was having financial difficulties," said Daisy. "My dealer told me he sold a sugar chest for Jay for nearly five thousand dollars."

"A sugar chest?" Libba's brow wrinkled. "When was this?"

"I don't know. A few days ago. Why?"

"Because he had a gorgeous sugar chest in his apartment."

Two sets of eyebrows rose. Not mine. I already knew—more than I wanted to—about Libba's trip to Jay's apartment.

"When were you in his apartment?" There was a speculative look in Jinx's eyes.

"Last week. And you don't need to leer like that. It was perfectly boring."

"But not perfectly innocent?" asked Jinx.

"Nosy."

Jinx pursed her lips. "I don't understand why anyone would want a sugar chest. They're not useful anymore." Jinx had sold off generations of antiques and filled her home with Kjaerhom hammock chairs, Castiglioni lamps, a Verner Paton dining set, and

Milo Baughman couches and tables. New, modern, and frighteningly chic.

"The point of a sugar chest isn't that it's useful. The point is that it's been in a family for generations." I reviewed my cards. "One no-trump. What else has Jay sold, Daisy?"

She fixed her gaze on the cards in her hand and her face puckered. "The dealer didn't say. Just that he had. Pass."

"I want to know more about Libba's trip to Jay's apartment," said Jinx.

"Really, you don't." Libba looked up from her cards. "Two clubs. It was b.o.r.i.n.g."

Jinx snapped her cards closed. "Pass."

I glanced at my cards. "Two spades."

Daisy passed.

"Four spades," said Libba.

Jinx passed.

Given Libba's propensity to overstate her hand, I erred on the side of caution. "Pass."

Jinx played the ace of diamonds. "We live vicariously through you, Libba. Spill."

Libba laid down ten lovely points. I could have kissed her. She grinned at me then shifted her gaze to Jinx. "He was boring. Do I need to draw you a picture?"

Daisy tittered. "No wonder you broke up with him."

Jinx pursed her lips. "Do you remember Carrie Phillips?"

"Who?" Daisy shifted three cards from the right side of her hand to the left.

"Carrie Phillips. Her maiden name was McGregor."

Daisy frowned at her cards. "Not ringing any bells."

It wasn't for me either.

"She's older than we are. Her sister Lois is closer to our age."

"Lois?" Daisy tilted again.

"Yes, Lois." Jinx sounded annoyed.

"Lois McGregor?" Libba straightened the cards she'd laid on the table.

I repressed the urge to swat Libba's hand away. I needed to see those cards so I could create a game plan.

"Exactly," said Jinx. "Lois and Carrie."

"What about Carrie?" asked Daisy.

"Her husband was hit by a car."

Oh. My. I tightened my grip on the cards in my hand. "Carrie Phillips? What's her husband's name?"

"John."

Oh God. My ability to draw air into my lungs departed.

"Why don't we ever see them?" Daisy shifted cards—the same ones?—from the left side of her hand to the right.

"Lois got married and moved to Chicago. The man Carrie married is an accountant. I've heard he's tight as a tick. He won't pay for a country club."

"Where was he hit?" Somehow I managed to speak without air.

"The midsection, I'd imagine. I heard he's in ICU."

"There are terrible drivers out there." This from Daisy, a woman who'd driven her station wagon off the driveway and into the stream that meandered through the golf course not once but twice.

"I mean where was he?"

"Oh." Jinx wrinkled her nose. "Coming out of his office."

"Did the driver stop?" I asked.

"No," said Jinx.

"See! Terrible drivers." At least Daisy hadn't hit a person—yet.

I shifted my gaze to my cards. The hearts and the spades ran together. Both Charles Dix and John Phillips were the victims of hit-and-runs? Not likely. "Is he conscious?"

"I don't think so," said Jinx.

"Is anyone putting together dinners for Carrie?"

My friends gaped at me. I didn't take dinners. I sent flowers or ran errands or delivered store-bought pastries. People seemed to prefer that.

"What?" I snapped. "Aggie is a fabulous cook."

Jinx closed her eyes.

Libba dug in her purse.

Daisy reached over and patted my hand.

I ground my teeth. Since that one incident, my friends didn't even let me bring side dishes to potluck. Who knew one wasn't supposed to cook the rice before mixing it with the soup in the casserole? Besides, it wasn't *that* mushy...

"I don't know if anyone has arranged meals." Jinx tapped the tips of her nails on the arm of her chair. "We don't really know her well enough."

Jinx was right. We didn't know Carrie well enough. It wasn't as if Aggie could whip up a dinner for me to take to the Phillips. What was I going to do? Knock on the door, hand Carrie a casserole, and ask about the attempt on her husband's life? I wouldn't recognize Carrie Phillips if she sat down at the bridge table with us.

Dammit.

Maybe Aggie could ask around...

Did Anarchy know?

"Let go of my arm." The voice was far too loud. We swiveled our heads and stared at the door to the hallway.

A man's voice, lower decibels and quite unintelligible, answered.

"I know she's here." The woman's voice was louder still.

It sounded as if a wronged wife was about to confront a mistress. Having been a wronged wife, my heart went out to her. Too bad she didn't understand she was picking a fight in the worst possible place. I shook my head and returned my gaze to the cards on the table. The kindest thing to do was mind my own business. Besides, I was not interested in anyone else's drama. I had enough of my own. I pulled the two of diamonds from the board. "Daisy?"

"What?" She shifted her attention back to the cards. "Oh, sorry. Here." A three of diamonds joined the ace and the two.

"Get your hands off me! Rape!"

Jinx pushed away from the table.

I folded my hand and put the cards down.

There would be no playing bridge until Jinx knew who was

causing such a scene. She stalked to the entry and stuck her head into the hallway.

"Where is she?" screeched the woman. "Where is Ellison Russell?"

FIFTEEN

Stormy Harney burst into the card room with all the force of a spring thunderstorm. Her parents had named her well. *Well* being a relative term.

She froze when she saw me. "Where is he?"

Unlike her brother, Stormy didn't hold a knife.

With her expression, she didn't need one.

If looks could kill, I'd already be dead.

My fingers turned to ice and I looked around the card room for a weapon. Nothing was available but a pair of brass candlesticks on the mantle and Daisy's purse—a bag which had the heft associated with a woman whose young children stowed everything from Matchbox cars to Golden Books within. Daisy's purse was closer and would probably do more damage. "Where is who?"

"You know who!"

Behind her, Reginald, one of the club's assistant managers, plucked at the fuzzy sleeve of her jacket. She ignored him. The man was as useful as a child's umbrella in a monsoon.

"No," I said. "I don't know of whom you are speaking."

"You think you're better than me. You're not." Her gaze took in our bridge game. "You're all just rich bitches."

Jinx, who stood next to the door, drew breath between her teeth. "Friend of yours, Ellison?"

Stormy might be right about one of the women.

"Reginald, perhaps you can see Mrs. Harney out?" I borrowed one of Mother's tones. The phrasing might suggest a question but the meaning was clear. Do it now.

Reginald blanched, but reached for Stormy's sleeve with the tips of his fingers as if he was concerned about catching something from the fake fur of her jacket.

She brushed him off like a weak mosquito. "Where is my brother? He went to see you and he hasn't come back."

"Ma'am, you're not allowed to wear denim here."

Stormy and I both shifted our gazes to Reginald. My gaze registered disbelief. Denim? His problem with Stormy was the dress code?

"Go to hell." Presumably, she was speaking to Reginald. Hard to tell since she'd returned her glare to me.

"Your brother attacked me with a knife. If you want to find him, I suggest you check the jails."

"That's a lie. Earl would never do that unless—"

Reginald closed his fingers around her arm.

"Unless he was high? He was. High as a kite."

"Bitch." Her hands curved into talons and she easily escaped Reginald's useless hold. She stalked forward looking as if she meant to rip my eyes from my head.

Daisy gasped.

I reached for the purse. "So much as touch me and you'll be arrested for assault."

She stepped closer. "I just want what's mine."

My fingers closed on the strap and I pulled it off the back of Daisy's chair. It thudded against the floor. Dear Lord, what did she have in there? Free weights? "I can't help you. You need to talk to a lawyer."

"I did." She scowled at me but at least she came no closer. "I went to one that Brooks knew. A silver-haired fast-talker. He said he wouldn't help me."

A silver-haired lawyer? Was that why Anarchy had questioned Hunter?

"You people all stick together."

I glanced at Jinx who was edging toward the door. Not all of us.

I hefted Daisy's purse into my lap.

"You're all working against me to make sure I don't get what's mine."

"You want Brooks' inheritance?" Daisy's brow furrowed and she tilted her head to the side. "But he died before he inherited."

"That's what she—" Stormy pointed an accusatory chipped talon at me "—said. I don't believe it. Brooks said that money was his."

"When he turned twenty-five." How many times had I explained this? "He hadn't yet turned twenty-five."

"It was his." Stormy was nothing if not stubborn.

"Is there something wrong with you? Are you stupid?" asked Jinx.

Stormy shifted the die-now glare to her.

Jinx didn't seem to notice. "This isn't difficult. The trust owned the money until Brooks' twenty-fifth birthday. He didn't reach his birthday."

"If you don't believe us, talk to the trust officer," said Libba. "His name is Jay Fitzhugh. I'd be happy to give you his number."

Libba had her revenge.

"I don't care who she talks to, she won't get a dime." Jinx crossed her arms.

"What about my baby?" Stormy laid her hand across her very flat stomach.

"You'll have to prove that it's his." Jinx was *not* being helpful.

"I'm his wife!"

"You were separated. His family didn't even know you existed."

"His family?" Stormy's throat produced a sound that might have been a laugh—that or a creaky sob. "You look down on me for wanting Brooks' money, but they want it just as much as I do."

True, but somewhere along the line a Harney had earned it.

Two beefy waiters appeared behind Reginald.

I jerked my head toward Stormy. Silly of me. The waiters were perfectly capable of seeing that the woman in the bell bottom jeans, platform sandals, flowered halter top, and coat that looked as if it could do double duty as shag carpet didn't belong.

One said, "Ma'am, you can walk out the door or we'll escort you out."

"Go to hell." She lunged toward me, knocking Libba out of her chair. Stormy's hands reached for me. Her body scattered the dummy hand and the cards we'd all laid down.

Dammit. Libba and I had had that game for sure.

I stood. "Libba?"

"I'm still among the living."

Thank God. Daisy's purse pulled on my arm. I'd swing it if I had to. Somehow. "I am not part of this, and I don't want any more trouble."

Stormy spit at me. A glistening globule that hung in the air before splatting against the ultrasuede tablecloth.

Ick.

One of the waiters grabbed the back of Stormy's jacket. The second clasped what looked to be a vice-like grip around her upper arm. "This way, ma'am."

"No." She locked her legs. "I'm not going anywhere. Not till you tell me where Earl is."

"I have no idea."

The men pulled—dragged—her away from the table.

She struggled against them. Her face reddened and her eyes narrowed to slits. "This whole mess is your fault."

My fault? All I'd done was find Brooks. She'd married him. A clown had killed him. None of this was my fault. "How?" I demanded.

"You doubted I was married to Brooks."

"We all doubted that." Libba's voice floated up from the floor.

Stormy kicked at her and missed. The waiters jerked her toward the door.

"Libba, are you all right?" I rounded the table with Daisy's purse pulling my arm out of its socket.

Libba sat on the floor with her skirt pushed several inches past decency and grinned. "Fine. I'll be able to dine out on this for months."

"This is a joke to you?" Stormy's face was as crimson as Daisy's BMW, which is to say garnet red. Spit clung to the corners of her mouth. She yanked uselessly against the waiters' holds. "You'll be sorry."

The waiters dragged her from the room and into the hallway. The string of expletives that spilled from Stormy's lips would have made a sailor blush—hell, they would have made Mistress K blush.

I offered Libba a hand, pulled her off the floor, and we followed Stormy and the waiters into the hall.

Well-coiffed heads popped out of rooms as Stormy told me to complete anatomically impossible feats. Mother would hear about this. Daddy might, too.

I let Daisy's purse fall to the wood floor. It sounded as if I'd dropped an anvil. "What do you have in there?"

"My youngest has been collecting pennies. We rolled them last night."

Thank God I hadn't swung Daisy's purse at Stormy. I might have killed her.

"Okay, here's the story." My gaze traveled from Libba to Daisy. They were no problem. I stared at Jinx longer. "I questioned whether or not that woman was actually married to Brooks Harney and she went crazy."

"When?" asked Jinx.

"Just now, didn't you see her?"

"No." Jinx shook her head. "When did you question her?"

"In the parking lot after the service." A convenient lie, so much easier than telling her my housekeeper was once a private investigator of sorts. I scratched my nose, caught Libba's eye, and dropped my hand to my side.

"Well, the woman is obviously four or five cards short of a full deck," said Jinx.

"Exactly." Libba smoothed her skirt. "I don't know about you girls, but I could use a drink."

"Isn't it a bit early?" asked Daisy.

"No." Three voices spoke in unison.

A new tablecloth, fresh cards, lunch, a glass of wine, several hours and three rubbers of bridge later, we got up from the card table and walked toward the exit.

I paused next to the ladies' lounge. "You girls go ahead. I need to stop."

We hugged and air-kissed and waved goodbye.

Moments later, I stepped into the parking lot. Given the beautiful day, it was nearly full with golfers' cars—Mercedes, a mid-life-crisis Porsche, Cadillacs, Volvos, three Jaguars, my Triumph, and, five spots away, a late-model, rust-spotted Cutlass with a dented fender and California plates.

My feet, quite of their own volition, stopped moving.

Was that Stormy's car?

She should have been long gone.

Was she waiting to attack me? My heart fluttered.

And what about my car? Had Stormy fiddled with the brakes or the steering?

Where was she?

The spaces between the cars morphed into hiding places.

I took one step forward and then another.

No one with a knife jumped out at me.

Emboldened, I took several more steps. Hurried steps. Please-don't-let-a-crazy-woman-with-a-knife-surprise-me steps.

A sharp noise cracked the air. The thwack of a well-hit golf ball or the sound of a gun cocking? Dread chilled my spine and fingers and toes. I scanned the parking lot. No one. But the gorgeous day seemed like a mask behind which danger lurked.

"Ellison!"

I jumped ten feet straight into the air.

"What's wrong? Are you okay?" Bill Humphrey, an old friend of Henry's, walked toward me.

I pressed my hand against my racing heart and gulped a lung's full of air. Yes, Bill was Henry's friend (definitely a strike against him) but at least he wasn't Stormy. "Bill, you startled me."

"I'm sorry." He sounded genuinely contrite. "I haven't seen you in a while. How have you been?"

He meant without Henry. That really wasn't a problem. "I'm muddling through."

"You look pale."

"My car won't start," I blurted. That made two lies in three hours but lying was better than barreling into a tree for lack of brakes or steering. "Could I prevail upon you for a ride home?"

"What's wrong with your car?" He frowned, presumably measuring the generous distance that still remained between me and the Triumph.

"I tried earlier and it wouldn't turn." Yet another lie. My nose itched like hell.

"Did you flood the engine? Let me try." He held out his hand for the keys.

For all I knew, Stormy had planted a bomb and the car would blow up when started. "No. Don't worry about it, Bill. I'll call the auto club."

His extended hand didn't move. "Don't be silly. Let me try. I insist."

"Really, it's all right. I'll call."

"Ellison, give me the keys."

Another man who wanted to manage me?

"No. Thank you. It's kind of you to offer but no."

He shrugged and shook his head, apparently writing me off as a silly female. "Suit yourself."

I planned to.

I hurried back to the clubhouse, slipped into a phone booth, and collapsed on the bench seat. I stared at the phone for a moment then, wishing I could come up with a better plan, I hit the button for an outside line and dialed.

Maybe he'd be out.

If he was, I'd call a cab then have a mechanic check the car over before I drove it.

Maybe I should just do that—

"Jones."

I swallowed. "Anarchy—"

"What now, Ellison?" He sounded tired. Of me.

Maybe I shouldn't bother him—

"What?"

"Um..." I swallowed again. When had my mouth gone so dry? "I'm at the club. Stormy Harney tracked me down here and threatened me. I'm worried she did something to my car."

"Don't go near it. I'm on my way."

He hung up before I could thank him or say goodbye.

I returned the receiver to the cradle and pushed myself off the bench. My joints and muscles ached as if I'd run ten miles instead of walked across a parking lot.

I emerged from the booth and flagged down a waiter. "May I please have glass of water?"

"Of course, Mrs. Russell. I'll bring that right out to you." He disappeared behind a swinging door where only staff ventured.

I waited, sinking into a flame stitch wingback.

The waiter returned with the water. "Are you sure you wouldn't like something stronger?"

I took the glass from his hands and read his nametag. "No, thank you, Tim."

I didn't sip the water. I gulped. I drained the glass and put it down on a table that held a *People Magazine*—apparently Burt Reynolds and Dinah Shore had decided not to get married and an Arkansas congressman had been canoodling with a stripper. I didn't need to read about having cold feet or cheating husbands. I was intimately familiar with both. Funny. The club usually had copies of financial newspapers or *Town and Country* on the tables. Maybe that *People* was a sign.

I shifted my gaze to the front window and waited for Anarchy to arrive.

I didn't wait long.

He must have put the siren thingy on the top of his car to arrive so quickly. It wasn't there now, but the unmarked police car still stood out like a sore thumb in a parking lot filled with imports. Well, not as much as the car with California plates.

I trotted outside and knocked on the window of Anarchy's car.

He opened the door. "What happened?"

"I was playing bridge with friends, and Stormy appeared and threatened me." I glanced toward her car. "She was escorted out of the club, but her car is still here."

"How long ago did you have her thrown out?"

"I didn't have her thrown out." Not exactly. "She wasn't in compliance with the dress code."

Anarchy's face contorted as if he was trying very hard not to roll his eyes.

I glanced at my watch. "It's been at least three hours since she was asked to leave."

He nodded and walked toward the car with California plates.

I followed him.

He peered through the driver's side window.

I did too.

A patchwork denim shoulder bag rested on the passenger seat.

Anarchy eased the car door open and reached for the bag.

"Is it hers?"

He couldn't help himself. He rolled his eyes. He also stuck his hand into the bag and withdrew a worn leather billfold.

He opened that and pulled out a driver's license. "Stormy Mack."

"Not Harney?"

He shook his head and showed me a driver's license with Stormy's picture. Her face was fuller and the haunted, hunted look in her eyes was absent.

He scanned the card. "Expired."

He would notice an infraction right off.

"She was escorted out?" he asked.

I nodded.

"By whom?"

"Two waiters. Reginald, the assistant manager, supervised."

"I'll need to speak with them. Where's your car?"

I pointed five spots down.

"Do you know how to pop the hood?"

"Of course." What was one more lie?

He pursed his lips as if he could tell I'd fibbed. "Give me the keys."

He could definitely tell. I handed over the keys.

Anarchy popped the hood, eyed the engine, closed the hood, and dropped to the pavement where he scooted on his back until his head and part of his shoulders were under the car.

He scooted into the open. "Your car is fine." He stood and returned my keys.

"Thank you." I looked around the parking lot. Anywhere but his eyes. "I played bridge today."

"Oh?" He sounded slightly bored. As a man, he didn't understand the sheer volume of information that could be gleaned at a bridge table.

"I heard John Phillips was hit by a car."

"Oh?"

"It can't be a coincidence. Do you have any leads?"

His eyes narrowed. "You ask a lot of questions." Translation: he had no intention of answering.

"You're not going to tell me?"

He answered with a quirk of his lips and a quick, decisive shake of his head.

Dammit. "Well then, here's another question for you."

He raised a brow.

"Where did Stormy Harney go without her purse or her car?"

SIXTEEN

Anarchy followed me home.

If he had any thoughts on my parking the Triumph in the garage instead of its customary spot in the circle drive, he kept them to himself. Sort of. "We need to talk," he said.

Nothing pleasant has ever followed those words. A thoroughly unpleasant melting sensation took hold of my intestines. "Fine. Come in." I unlocked the backdoor and stepped into the kitchen.

Anarchy followed me inside. "Where's Aggie?"

"It's Tuesday. She's doing the marketing."

"And Grace?"

I glanced at the clock on the stove. "She'll be home shortly."

"And Max?"

The dog ambled in and yawned big enough so that even Mr. Magoo could see past his tonsils and into his stomach, then he rubbed his head against my leg.

I scratched behind his ears. "Have you been sleeping on my bed, you naughty dog? Do you want to go out?" I wasn't above using my dog to delay a conversation I didn't want to have.

Max wagged his stubby tail.

I held the door open for him. He meandered outside and sniffed around the yard, looking for the absolute perfect place to relieve himself. *Take your time.*

"Ellison." Anarchy's hand brushed against my shoulder. Did he feel my muscles tense?

I didn't turn. "Wait a minute. If he sees a rabbit, he'll be gone."

For once, Max completed his business and trotted immediately back to the house. Drat. Couldn't he chase a squirrel or investigate the back neighbor's fence? Nope. He wanted a biscuit.

I handed over a dog treat. "Would you care for anything to drink? I can make coffee." Mr. Coffee sat ready and waiting to do exactly as I asked. *He* never asked to have awkward conversations.

"Nothing. Thank you."

I opened the refrigerator door and moved things around. The ketchup ought to be next to the mustard not the milk.

"Ellison." Anarchy's voice held an edge.

I grabbed a Tab and a lime and turned to face him. "What?"

He leaned against the counter, cool beyond words, handsome beyond belief.

"I know, I know. You want to know why Stormy Harney showed up at the country club."

He scowled. "I want to know what's going on with you."

I tightened my grip on the Tab, denting the can. "Nothing."

"That's not true." He moved toward me. I didn't budge. I couldn't. Bumps on logs had stronger wills than I did. Anarchy ran the tip of his finger along the line of my jaw, setting off all sorts of shivery sensations in places that had no business shivering over a man's touch. "Tell me."

"The truth?"

"No." He grinned. "Lie to me."

He wanted the truth? Fine. "Every man I know—" I shot an apologetic glance at blameless Mr. Coffee "—wants to run my life."

"That's not true."

"It is." I took a sip of Tab. I had to. The dryness in my mouth threatened to turn my tongue to dust.

"I don't tell you what to do."

I choked on a sip of Tab. "You told me to stay away from Stormy and your investigation."

"I don't want you to get hurt. And I'd tell anyone who's not a cop the same thing."

"Really?" Sarcasm twisted my voice into something unpleasant.

"Really." His voice was matter-of-fact. He believed what he was saying. "Has Tafft been forcing you to do things?" Now his voice held an edge.

"No."

"Then who?"

I crossed my arms and backed away. "I don't want to discuss this."

Anarchy was stuck. If he forced the issue, he was just one more man telling me what to do—or in this case, what to talk about. "That husband of yours really did a number on you."

Wanting to stand on my own two feet wasn't about Henry. It wasn't about my past. It was about my future.

"What if I promise not to tell you what to do?" His eyes twinkled.

I shook my head. "You can't help yourself."

"I bet I can." His finger returned to my jaw and his touch nearly melted my resolve.

"You can't." Even as the words left my mouth, part of my brain wanted them back. Just as part of my body wanted to fall into his arms and let him take care of me—chances were he'd do a bang up job. I took a step backward. Away from him.

His lips thinned. "I figured I'd spend the next year or so competing with Tafft." His hand reached toward me. I didn't need another case of the shivers. I took another step back.

"I don't know how to compete with this." His voice was soft.

"With me wanting to be an independent woman?"

He offered me half of a smile. "Are you going to roar?"

"I might."

Now I got the full smile in all its bone-melting glory. And his eyes...why did they have to be the exact shade of coffee? He was making this whole independent woman thing difficult. Chances were he knew it.

Brnng, brnng.

Thank God. I snatched the phone from the cradle.

"Hello."

"You were wrong." A woman's voice traveled down the phone line.

"Who is this?"

"You were wrong."

"You already said that." I was not in the mood for games. "Who's calling?"

"Brooks' brother just offered me ten thousand dollars to go away. He wouldn't have done that if I didn't have a claim on Brooks' inheritance." Stormy Harney. I'd had visions of her dead and buried in a sand trap. Not hardly. Her voice held a na-na-boo-boo quality that set my teeth on edge.

And Robbie Harney was an idiot.

"When did you see Robbie?"

"I saw him in the parking lot at your club." She spat the last word. "He took me out for a drink and made his offer."

"If I were you, I'd take the money and run."

Across from me, Anarchy raised a brow.

"I want what I came for," said Stormy.

"I thought you came for Brooks. That you wanted to win him back."

"That's what I just said."

"No. It's not. You said you came for his money." Had she killed him to get it? It wasn't much of a stretch—no stretch at all—to imagine Earl dressed in a clown suit.

"You twist everything around. Besides, it doesn't matter. Brooks is dead."

I had no response to that and a silence fell between us.

"What's the man's name?"

"What man?"

"The trust officer. The one your friend told me about."

"Jay Fitzhugh."

"I'm going to call him. He'll hand over the money."

"You should." Maybe when Jay made it clear she'd never see a dime of the Harney fortune, Stormy would take Robbie's offer and go back to California.

"Where can I reach him?"

I gave her the name of the bank. "Do you want the number?"

"I have a phone book." She sounded as spiteful as a five-year-old denied ice cream. Then I heard a dial tone.

I stared at the receiver in my hand. "She hung up on me."

"Stormy Harney?" asked Anarchy.

His question was probably rhetorical, but I nodded anyway. "I left a message about her for you. Did you get it? Brooks asked her for a divorce."

"I got the message, but she has an alibi for the night he was killed."

"What about her brother?"

Anarchy donned an unreadable expression—his cop face. "I'm not telling you what to do, but as a favor to me, would you please stay away from those people?"

"I will." It was an easy promise to make. I wanted nothing more to do with Stormy or her knife-wielding brother. "I promise."

A repetitive clunking thud carried through the closed backdoor.

"What's that?" he asked

"Bessie. Aggie's home." I opened the backdoor and started out.

"Where are you going?"

"She's been to the store. I'm going to help her carry groceries in."

"You help your housekeeper with the groceries?"

That was not worth a response. I walked outside and took a bag from Aggie's arms.

"That cop is here," she whispered.

That cop. It's not that Aggie dislikes Anarchy. She'd just rather see me with Hunter.

"Be nice," I whispered back.

"When am I not?"

"Good point."

We entered the kitchen where Anarchy had resumed his slouchy, arms crossed, brown eyes more seductive than coffee pose.

Aggie didn't seem to notice. "Good afternoon, detective." Her voice was crisp, business-like.

"Good afternoon. May I take that for you?" He plucked a bag of groceries from Aggie's arms and put it on the counter.

"Thank you." She returned to the door. "There's another bag in the car." Out she went, leaving me alone with Anarchy. The silence between us itched.

"I should get going," he said.

I didn't argue. "Thank you for helping me."

"You can call me anytime you need me."

I blinked.

"I'm willing to wait for what I want." He rubbed his jaw reminding me how his fingers felt on *my* jaw. "For who I want."

Ding dong.

Saved by the bell. Thank God. "I should answer that."

Together we walked down the front hall and into the foyer. I pulled open the front door. My father stood on the other side.

He noticed Anarchy and his eyes narrowed. "What's happened now?"

"Nothing." That really wasn't a lie.

"Oh? I heard Brooks Harney's widow accosted you at the club."

"She's just frustrated because she can't get her mitts on Brooks' money."

"So she did accost you?" My father looked annoyed, missed-an-easy-putt-and-lost-the-club-tournament annoyed.

"No. She yelled at me. That's all." She'd accosted Libba but since that—for the most part—had been unintentional I saw no need to mention it.

"We need to talk. Would you please excuse us, detective?" It was a dismissal.

Anarchy studied us both then he nodded at me. Curtly. "Of course." He slipped through the front door.

My father glared at me. "You get into trouble everywhere you go."

That was a gross exaggeration. I glared back. "I do not."

"I want you safe."

"I appreciate that. I do. But I'm not getting married again so you don't have to worry about me."

"That's not why I want you to get married."

"Oh?"

"A good marriage would bring you happiness and security and—" he glanced around the foyer with its bombe chest topped by a bouquet of mums, gleaming hardwoods, and crystal chandelier "—stability."

If he'd asked me, I would have told him I was already plenty happy, secure, and stable.

"I don't want to get married." Especially not for those reasons. If I ever said "I do" again it would be because I was in love.

His brows drew together. Given his patrician features, I felt like the establishment was frowning at me. "Did you talk to your sister?"

"I did."

"And?"

"I told her how you felt."

"You didn't talk her out of the operation?"

"No. It's her choice. We should respect it."

"Listen, Sugar. You two are my little girls—"

"We're not. We're adults. We have families. We have daughters of our own."

"You're still my little girls. I still want to protect you."

How to convince him that his job as a father wasn't to protect us, it was to teach us how to protect ourselves? "You're going to have to trust that we can protect ourselves."

"Like the other night? A man held a knife to your throat."

This debate of ours was going nowhere. That or my father was winning. In either case, it needed to stop.

"I'm very grateful that you and Mother happened along." We both knew it was Mother who'd insisted they drive to my house for an explanation. There was no way my father, left to his own devices, would have roused himself on a Friday night to search for the reason Hunter Tafft had been led out of the club party.

"I love you, Ellie."

"Then have some faith in me."

That earned me another scowl.

Aggie stuck her head full of sproingy curls into the foyer. "I'm sorry to interrupt, but Olivia Forde is on the phone. She'd like to come at ten instead of eleven. Is that all right?"

I hadn't even heard the phone ring. "Fine."

"Olivia Forde?" asked my father.

"She's a decorator. I've decided to redo Henry's study."

My father grunted his approval. Decorating—or redecorating—was a legitimate way for a woman to spend her time.

"Could you try and understand my point? Please?" I walked toward Henry's study and the telephone. "I'm an adult."

He shook his head. "Try and understand mine. You're my daughter. It's my job to look out for you."

It was time he retired.

Olivia Forde stood in the exact center of the study and turned a slow circle on the sensible heels of her Ferragamos. Those flats were a surprise. I'd expected any decorator Libba recommended to be impossibly chic. Not Olivia. In addition to her flats she wore a twin set and a plaid skirt. Like her shoes, she looked sensible—the type of woman with whom I might enjoy sharing a bottle of wine. "The carpet will have to go."

And she had good taste.

"Agreed."

"And the walls. Do you want to paint the paneling?"

"Absolutely not. Can we have it sanded and stained a lighter color?"

She nodded. "Of course, but that will cost you."

"No paint."

"I agree."

Of course she did. She'd just added to her bill.

"What about a light pecan shade?"

"You're the decorator."

"Yes, but you're an artist. If you're not happy with the color, you won't be happy with the room."

No wonder she was developing a mile-long client list.

"I'm in no hurry. Have the walls sanded then stain a swatch the color you think would work. If I like it, we'll continue with the whole room. If not, we'll try again."

She jotted something on a legal pad. "About the floor."

"There are hardwoods underneath. I imagine they're in good shape."

She glanced down at Henry's horrid carpet. "May I?"

"Of course."

She crossed to a corner of the room, withdrew a pocketknife from her handbag, crouched, and pulled back a piece of the rug.

In my experience, looking under the carpet—granted mine was metaphorical (usually)—led to nothing but trouble. I avoided peeking whenever possible.

Olivia had no such qualms. "You're right. They look good." She stood. "What else did you have in mind?"

"I have an antique Sarouk in storage."

Her eyes widened. "Colors?"

"The center medallion is light blue and the field is indigo. As I remember there are green and persimmon spandrels."

She smiled her approval. "It sounds lovely."

"It is. I always thought it would be perfect in here but Henry wanted shag."

She pointed to a ten-foot expanse where our last decorator had grouped English hunting prints above a library table. "What about that wall?"

"What about it?"

"With the right art it could be a focal point."

Our last decorator couldn't believe I didn't want my own paintings in every room. I still didn't. That hadn't changed.

"Like what?"

"I have two Chinese tapestries. Matching, of course."

"Of course."

"I bought them from a dealer in Chicago." She paused, probably waiting for me to coo or be impressed with her connections in a larger city.

I didn't. I wasn't.

"They're a lovely cream silk," she continued. "A garden scene. The first is of a woman standing on a balcony overlooking a garden. The second is more of the garden with flowers and birds and wildlife."

They sounded beautiful...and familiar. "Are the colors primarily blue and persimmon with sage, emerald, and gold accents?"

"Exactly. How did you know?"

"A friend of my grandmother's has tapestries just like that."

"Really?" A furrow appeared between Olivia's brows. "I was assured these were one-of-a-kind. Perhaps she sold them."

"Doubtful. They were a family heirloom."

"Well, these are exquisite."

"If they're anything like PeeWa's, I'm sure they are. When I was a little girl, I would beg to go with my grandmother whenever she went to PeeWa's house. I'd sit in front of those tapestries for hours and look at the colors and the expression on the woman's face and the way the birds looked as if they were ready to swoop off the silk."

"Shall I bring them by?"

"Absolutely."

"If you like them, we can lay your Sarouk, hang them there." She waved away Henry's hunting prints. "Get rid of the desk." She raised a brow, testing to see if I had any objections to banishing the ponderous piece of furniture.

I didn't.

"Perhaps you could sell it for me."

She nodded then her gaze shifted to the leather club chairs, too deep for a woman to sit in comfortably. "What about more feminine chairs? Maybe covered in cream linen?"

"Perfect."

When Olivia Forde left, I called Mother.

"You talked to your father." It wasn't a question. It was an accusation.

"I did."

"You made things worse."

I didn't argue. "I have a question for you."

"What?"

"Do you remember the oriental screens PeeWa Asbury had hanging in her sitting room?" Née Penelope Warren Blake, her first and middle names had been mashed together for a childhood nickname that saw her through her whole life.

"Of course I remember. Your grandmother used to insist on taking you to see them. I was scared to death you were going to touch them and mar the silk or knock a piece of Lalique off a side table. She had crystal ashtrays everywhere."

"The silk was behind glass."

"You could have smudged it."

A million smart replies came to mind. I uttered none of them. "Remind me. Where did the tapestries come from?"

"PeeWa's mother was English. The story is that her father—PeeWa's grandfather—picked them up when he was stationed in Hong Kong."

"Did she sell them?"

"Sell them?" The incredulous tone of Mother's voice told me that was about as likely as PeeWa flying to the moon on one wing.

"My decorator just described something remarkably similar."

"What are you decorating?"

"The study."

"Are you sure you're ready to do that?"

More than ready. "About the tapestries—"

"Go visit PeeWa. She'd love to see you. I'm quite sure the tapestries are still hanging in her sitting room." She paused. "Oh.

Wait. She's not at home. She's in assisted living. You should still go see her."

"At Carlyle Place?"

"Where else? About you and your father—"

"Mother, I have to go. Love you. Bye." I hung up the phone before we could rehash that conversation a third time. Then I sat and stared at the too dark walls of Henry's study. I was being silly. There were probably hundreds, if not thousands, of tapestries exactly like the ones I'd fallen in love with at PeeWa's. So why did I feel as if something was wrong?

SEVENTEEN

Carlyle Place. A patrician name. It sounded as if it should be nestled in the mountains of Palm Springs or Scottsdale. Or perhaps Carlyle Place should have faced east, stalwart against Atlantic gales but open to ocean breezes from Newport or Palm Beach.

Carlyle Place sat on a hill not far from the Plaza.

It got full credit for looking like a fine old home—parquet floors, lovely drapes, fresh flowers in crystal vases on practically every surface. But beneath the scents of lemon furniture polish and stargazer lilies lurked a more clinical odor.

I followed an attractive young woman to PeeWa's suite and knocked on the door.

No one answered.

"She may not have her hearing aids in." The woman knocked again. Louder this time.

There was still no response.

She opened the door and stuck her head inside. "Mrs. Asbury? It's Alice. You have a visitor." Her voice had the sing-song quality I associated with talking to toddlers. She stepped inside. "Mrs. Asbury?"

I followed her directly into a sitting room.

Someone had decorated PeeWa's suite with treasures from her home. I recognized a chair she'd once assured me came to Kansas City on a covered wagon. Framed photographs hung on the walls—PeeWa and her husband Kenneth. PeeWa and her son Kenny who'd died in France fighting Germans. PeeWa and my grandmother,

Lillian. The evening newspaper lay on a coffee table. Next to it sat a still steaming cup of coffee.

"Mrs. Asbury?" Alice raised her voice a decibel or two. She crossed the small living room, walked down a short hallway, and opened the door to what was presumably the bedroom. "Where are you?"

Flush.

The sound of running water followed.

A moment passed then the door in the hallway opened and PeeWa emerged wearing an enormous evening suit and a strand of pearls that seemed to weigh on her neck. Her fluffy white hair looked freshly styled and too big for her head. PeeWa had shrunk. She noticed us and frowned.

"We have a visitor," said Alice. "Isn't that lovely?"

PeeWa's frown deepened to a scowl. "I'm quite sure *we* do not have a visitor. I have a visitor. You may leave."

Alice smiled sweetly, apparently immune to sharp tongues. "Call if you need anything."

PeeWa's scowl disappeared with Alice. "What a treat it is to see you, dear. May I offer you coffee?"

"Thank you." I never turn down coffee.

"I still make it the old way. There's a French press on the counter in the kitchen. Do you mind helping yourself?"

"Of course not." I entered the tiny kitchen and took a delicate cup and saucer from the cabinet. Meissen? I turned over the cup. Right in one. The pattern was Ming dragon. PeeWa loved all things Chinese. I poured my coffee and joined her on the couch.

She patted my knee. "I have plans this evening so I can't talk long. Tell me all your news. How have you been?"

"How have *you* been?"

"Fine. Playing lots of bridge. Kenny is coming soon. He's going to take me to the opera."

I blinked. "Kenny?"

"Yes, dear. Kenny. My son." She leaned back against the couch. "He takes such good care of me."

I took a sip of my coffee. It wasn't nearly strong enough. "Which opera?"

"Bizet's Carmen."

PeeWa was right about the current production, but who was taking her to the opera? Was anyone taking her?

"I haven't seen Kenny in years. Remind me what he looks like."

"His picture is right there on the wall." She pointed to a photograph. "Of course, he's a bit older now. We all are." She regarded me with faded blue eyes. "Except you. You haven't aged a day."

"Thank you. What time is Kenny picking you up?"

She opened her mouth then closed it, tilted her head, then regarded a grandfather clock in the corner. "Go ask Alice. She'll know. Now...enough about me. How's Frances?"

"She's fine, thank you."

"And Ellison, how is she?"

The aide's name might be Alice, but I was the one who'd fallen down the rabbit hole. "I'm fine."

"You already told me that. How's your granddaughter?"

I pasted on a bright smile. Did Mother know about this? If so, she should have shared. "Ellison is painting a lot. Her daughter Grace is a sophomore in high school."

"Is she still married to that awful man? The one you didn't like."

My grandmother hadn't liked Henry?

"He died."

"Did he? I forgot. I imagine she's happier without him."

Was I happy? I was glad Henry was out of my life, but was I happy alone? That was a question for later. I glanced around PeeWa's sitting room. "This is a lovely room."

"Isn't it?" She sat back against the couch and admired.

"Ellison was always so fond of those Chinese panels." It felt odd talking about myself in third person. "Do you still have them?"

"Of course." She sounded offended that I—or Lillian—had even suggested such a thing. "My grandfather brought them back from China. I'd never part with those."

"Are they at the house?"

PeeWa's blue eyes clouded and she looked around her little sitting room as if she wasn't quite sure where she was. "Of course. Go look at them." She pointed toward the front door.

Poor PeeWa. My heart contracted and I paused, waiting until I was sure my voice wouldn't shake. "I will in a bit. Tell me more about Kenny."

She sighed, a happy sound. "He insists on taking me out at least once a week. Sometimes we go to Winstead's. You know how I love chocolate frosties."

I did. As a child, PeeWa and my grandmother took me there whenever they needed a chocolate fix—that is to say, often.

"Tonight he's taking me to the opera."

A band tightened around my chest. Time had worn away the sharp edges of PeeWa's mind, leaving her a blurred version of the woman she used to be. She might not notice. I hoped she didn't notice. "What a treat." Who was Kenny? Was there anyone coming or would she sit alone in her suite and wait?

"Isn't it? I haven't been feeling up to snuff, and it's so important to have family around when times are tough."

My jaw ached with the effort of not crying.

Knock, knock.

"That must be him now." She squeezed my knee. "Come in." Her voice trilled.

The door opened and a smile of sheer delight lit her face. "Kenny, you're here. You remember my friend, Lillian, don't you?"

Hunter Tafft stepped inside. He paused when he saw me then approached the couch and dropped a soft kiss on PeeWa's wrinkled cheek. "You look lovely." He turned to me. "Lillian, it's nice to see you."

"Likewise."

"Kenny," said PeeWa. "Lillian was just asking about the Chinese tapestries. You'll show them to her won't you?"

"Of course." He held out his hand. "Lillian?"

I rose from the couch without his help. "PeeWa, you have tickets. I'll see the tapestries later. I'm going to run, but I'll visit you again soon."

"Don't be silly. I can wait. Go look. You know, Ellison adores them."

"I know."

Hunter held the door for me.

I paused in the doorway. "It was good to see you, PeeWa. I'll come again soon."

"When you come back, I want a jar of your face cream. You don't look a day over fifty."

Given that I hadn't yet hit forty, that wasn't particularly flattering. "I will."

Hunter followed me into the hall. "What are you doing here?"

"I could ask you the same thing."

His mouth thinned. "We're cousins."

Of course they were. I'd forgotten. Then again, if I went back a few generations, I could count half the people I knew as cousins.

"She's lonely. Her husband and her son are gone. Her sister is in Dallas. If I don't take her out, she's here all day, every day."

That might be true—probably was true—but Hunter Tafft was, as Mother constantly reminded me, a busy man. That he chose to spend some of his free time treating an old woman to steakburgers and chocolate frosties made my heart melt.

My heart had no business melting.

"I want to make sure she's being taken care of. Why are you here?"

"It's probably nothing, but..."

"But what?"

I glanced inside PeeWa's suite. She waited patiently on the couch. Was she really hard of hearing or had she ignored the knock on her door to annoy Alice? "A decorator offered me Chinese panels that sounded exactly like the ones in PeeWa's sitting room," I whispered. "I wondered if she had sold them."

"She hasn't. She'd never part with them."

I nodded. "When I asked, she said the same thing."

"You think someone stole them?"

"The thought had crossed my mind."

"I'll run by the house tomorrow and make sure everything is all right."

"What time are you going?"

"Why?" He frowned at me.

"I practically grew up at her house. I can tell you if anything else is missing."

"You think the panels are gone."

The sick feeling in my stomach said yes. I hoped my stomach was wrong.

I sat on the top step of PeeWa's front stoop, glad I'd worn a warm coat. Sharp gusts of wind ripped leaves from the trees and made my eyes water. The kiddos would be wearing jackets over their costumes tonight for sure.

When she was little, Grace *hated* that. She wanted everyone in the neighborhood to see her princess costume, not her new winter coat. Henry always volunteered to take the neighborhood kids around. He'd lead a pack of cowboys and ghosts and princesses, waiting on the sidewalk as the kids ran from house to house.

I stayed home and handed out candy. I also made hot chocolate and kept it warm on the stove. Two things were certain. Grace would come home with enough candy to keep her satisfied till Easter, and she'd be shivering with cold. Somewhere between the Parkersons' and the Clarendons', she'd pass her coat to her father.

He let her. Every time. Henry might not have cared much about my happiness, but he cared desperately about Grace's. He'd have done almost anything to bring a smile to her face.

Of course he wasn't the one who took care of her three days later when she came down with a violent cold.

A Mercedes pulled up the drive, parked behind my Triumph, and brought my thoughts back to the present.

Hunter got out of the car. "It's cold out here."

"Yes."

"Why didn't you wait in your car?"

"I needed some air." I stood.

Hunter pulled a keychain with but one key from his pocket, slotted the key in the lock, and opened the door.

I stepped inside. The air was stale and chilly.

"The furnace man was out at the beginning of the month. I'll turn on the heat."

"Don't bother. This won't take long." I took in PeeWa's foyer. It hadn't changed. A Chinese altar table with a carved apron and lion feet still held a Ming vase. An Aubusson rug still covered the floor. "This way."

I led Hunter through the living room to the right of the front hall. It opened onto PeeWa's sitting room.

Two comfortable chairs flanked a side table which held a good reading lamp. The table also held a stack of books, one with a bookmark emerging from the middle. PeeWa's chaise lounge sat near the window, more light, more books, and a stunning view of her panels.

When I was a girl, I stretched out on that chaise and gazed at the garden scene on the wall.

Except now the garden scene wasn't there.

A large still life hung in the panels' place.

I glanced at Hunter. His cheeks had gone pale and his face looked as if it had been chiseled from marble.

"Who has keys to the house?" I asked.

He made a noise in his throat. It might have been a chuckle. It might have been a growl. "The gardener, the cleaning lady, the trust company, the Coes, the neighbors to the left, and the Helmricks, the backyard neighbors. Plus, PeeWa says there's a key hidden on the patio. I've never been able to find it." He pinched the bridge of his nose. "Who offered you the panels?"

"Olivia Forde. She's a decorator, and she bought them from a dealer in Chicago. At least that's what she told me."

"How well do you know this house?"

"I know the downstairs well. The upstairs not at all. Why?"

"We didn't inventory when we moved PeeWa to Carlyle Place."

"So you don't know exactly what was here."

"No." His voice was bleak. "Will you look around while I call the police?"

I determined that PeeWa's hand cooler collection was gone as was a Qing box made of Zitan wood with inlaid mother of pearl depicting a bird on a cherry tree branch. That box had been second in my affections after the panels.

We met in the kitchen. Like the rest of the house, it was chilly. I told Hunter what was missing then opened the cabinet closest to the sink and peered inside, then I opened another, and another. I wanted coffee like Brooks had once wanted a shot of heroine.

"What are you doing?" asked Hunter.

"Looking for coffee." Silly and I knew it. Any coffee I found would be stale.

"There isn't any."

"You're sure? I'd settle for instant."

"There's nothing. We emptied all the cupboards when we moved her." His handsome face looked ten years older, like he was a man actually old enough to have a head of silver hair.

I wasn't the only one who needed coffee.

Hunter pulled a small leather-bound notebook from inside his suit coat and picked up the phone.

"Who are you calling?"

"The bank."

"Why?"

His finger circled the dial. "Because they're co-executors." He finished dialing, waited a few seconds, then said, "Trust department, please." Seconds passed then he added, "Hunter Tafft calling, I need to speak with the officer responsible for PeeWa Asbury's trust."

His expression darkened. "Try Penelope Asbury." His gaze traveled the kitchen, from the coffee-free cabinets to the refrigerator to the stove to me.

I swallowed.

"I'll leave a message," he said to the person on the phone. "You're ready? This is Hunter Tafft. Mrs. Asbury's home has been burglarized." A pause. "Yes, I'm sure. I have her family friend Ellison Russell with me now, and she's identified several missing antiques."

He listened, an intent expression settling upon his face.

"I've called the police. They're on their way. Tell him I'll wait for him here." He hung up.

I glanced around PeeWa's empty kitchen and swallowed. "I played bridge."

"Oh?" Unlike Anarchy, Hunter didn't sound bored. He'd been married often enough to understand that table talk meant useful information.

"John Phillips was hit by a car. A hit and run, the same as Charles Dix."

He nodded, waiting.

"I'm telling you because theirs were the other cards Brooks slipped in my pocket."

"You're worried about me." His voice was velvet.

I was. "I just thought you should know. So you could look both ways when you cross the street."

Hunter's usually sharp gaze softened.

Ding dong.

Thank God. "I'll get it." I left Hunter in the kitchen and hurried to the front door.

Blessedly neither of the detectives on the other side was Anarchy Jones. They were paunchy and they sported unlikely mustaches and pouches beneath their eyes. Nothing like Anarchy—although one did wear plaid pants. He spoke first. "We got a call about a burglary."

"Won't you come in?"

"Who are you?" asked the detective with tan pants.

"Ellison Russell. And you are?"

"Detective Gilbert." He jerked his head toward his plaid-pants-wearing partner. "That's Detective Sullivan."

Seriously? "May I please see some identification?"

With long-suffering expressions, they stuck their badges in front of my nose. It was true. The police department had dispatched Gilbert and Sullivan to a crime scene. Who says cops don't have a sense of humor?

"If you start singing from the Mikado, we'll be forced to arrest you," said Detective Gilbert. He looked deadly serious.

"No singing." I opened the door wider and moved out of their way.

"What was taken?" Detective Sullivan pulled a pen and a steno pad from his jacket. He looked ridiculously out of place in PeeWa's foyer.

"Two Chinese screens, a box, and some hand coolers."

"Hand coolers?" asked Detective Gilbert.

"Yes. Hand coolers."

"What exactly is a hand cooler?"

"During the Victoria era, ladies' hands were expected to be cool and dry. They carried bits of porcelain or crystal to make sure they didn't have sweaty palms."

"Why would someone steal those?" asked Detective Sullivan.

"They're highly collectible."

Both detectives looked doubtful.

"PeeWa had a significant collection."

"PeeWa?" Gilbert cocked his head to the side.

"Penelope Asbury, the lady who owns the house."

"So, who are you?" Sullivan now wore a suspicious expression.

"A family friend."

Hunter chose that moment to enter the foyer. "I'm Hunter Tafft. I called."

"These are Detectives Gilbert and Sullivan," I said.

"Right."

The tone of Hunter's voice let me know what he thought of my joking around.

"Seriously."

"Are you also a family friend?" asked Detective Gilbert.

Detective Sullivan said nothing. There was a pinched look around his mouth that his mustache couldn't hide.

"I'm Mrs. Asbury's lawyer."

"Does anyone live here?"

"Not right now," said Hunter.

"But you came here today." Gilbert, unencumbered by a notepad, crossed his arms. He also raised a single brow.

There was no way a police detective was going to intimidate Hunter. "Yes."

"Why?"

"Someone offered to sell Mrs. Russell a pair of Chinese panels. She knew Mrs. Asbury owned a similar pair, knew they were rare, and alerted me to the possible theft."

"Who offered them to you, Mrs. Russell? A fence?"

Did I look like the kind of woman who went to pawn shops? I smoothed my hair and wished I'd taken time to don something dressier than jeans. "My decorator."

"His name?"

"Olivia Forde."

"How did Miss Forde come to have them?"

"A dealer in Chicago. You'd have to ask her."

Detective Sullivan looked at his notepad. "What about the box?"

"It was an antique. Museum quality."

"A box?" asked Gilbert.

I told them all about the box, described the inlay, the lining, the patina of the wood.

Sullivan looked up from his note taking. "Anything else missing?"

"I'm not sure. I haven't been here in years."

"Really?" Sullivan's eyes narrowed. Somehow, I'd earned his

suspicion. "The way you described that box, I'd think you saw it just yesterday."

I rubbed my suddenly stiff neck. "It was a favorite of mine as a child."

"If Mrs. Russell hadn't pointed out the box was missing, no one would have noticed it was gone." Hunter used one of his courtroom glares on the detectives. "She didn't take it."

Sullivan grunted.

That was it. I needed coffee. And after coffee, I needed to exercise. A run with Max would set me right.

"If you'll excuse me." I walked toward the living room.

"Where are you going?" asked Gilbert.

"To get my purse. I'm going home." I hummed "Three Little Maids." Loudly.

"You can't hold her," said Hunter.

"We'll need your fingerprints," said Sullivan.

I snatched my bag off the couch. "I'm sure they're on file. If you can't find them, just ask Anarchy Jones." With that, I sailed out the front door.

It's so seldom I get the last word, I relished it all the way home. I should have known all that relish would give me indigestion.

EIGHTEEN

There are three things a woman can depend upon—death, taxes, and Mr. Coffee. And of the three, Mr. Coffee is the only one I wanted to think about on a regular basis.

He served up a pot of coffee. Perfect. Fast. Replenishing.

I drank two cups.

I might have drunk three, but Max was weaving around my ankles like a ninety-pound cat.

I ceded. "Fine. We'll go for a run."

He wagged his stubby tail.

Ten minutes later, I laced up my Adidas and we walked down the drive at a quick pace.

Max tugged on the leash.

"Give me a minute to warm up."

He looked over his shoulder, his doggy expression reflecting what he thought of that idea.

I wasn't going to let one more disapproving male faze me. We walked for three blocks then broke into a slow jog.

Again Max shot a disgusted look over his shoulder. He wanted a sprint.

Not today.

We reached Loose Park and I increased my speed. Still not fast enough for Max—he had the energy to spot squirrels, eye other dogs, and stick his nose in the air to check for odd scents, all at the same time.

My thoughts fell into rhythm with my steps. Hopeless snarls smoothed to mere tangles. Who had stolen from PeeWa?

Most everyone I knew was aware that she was living at Carlyle Place. Anyone could have found the key hidden on her patio and helped themselves to her treasures. An ordinary thief would have taken the silver service or the television. This thief had cherry-picked her antiques, taking the most valuable among them. Who was it?

I'd look at the panels Olivia had. If they were PeeWa's, the police would be able to trace the thief through Olivia's dealer.

That thread reasonably straightened, my mind shifted to poor Brooks Harney. Who had killed him?

It was obviously over money. With so much involved, it had to be.

Had Earl stabbed him or had it been his brother?

That thought chilled my blood so much it matched the wind temperature.

I was missing something. I felt it in the tension in my shoulders and neck. Somewhere in the morass of thoughts in my brain lay the answer. If I chased it, it would run away. If I ignored it, there was a chance it would percolate to the surface.

Max tugged again.

The temptation to let him off his leash was terrible and the park was almost empty. But all I needed was for him to barrel into some little old lady out for her daily constitutional—rather like the one a few hundred feet in front of us. A dark coat covered her bent back and a nylon scarf covered her hair—more to protect it from the wind than to keep her warm. Her legs, covered with stockings, were stick thin and disappeared into those boots that every old lady of my acquaintance owned. The boots looked more like galoshes than actual boots, but they were fur-lined and very much *au courant* for the over-seventy set.

She looked like just the sort of lady Max might accidentally upend.

I tightened my hold on his leash.

Given that we were running and she was shuffling, we closed the distance quickly.

Too quickly.

There was the pond. I used to like the pond. When the weather was warm, ducks swam in the pond. Children gathered and fed them. There was picturesque bridge and a small island, both of which looked lovely in paintings.

I stopped liking the pond when I drove into it.

Even now I scowled at its placid waters.

Max tugged again.

That's when I saw it. The older lady was not alone. A Yorkie walked next to her.

Most of the time Max was too smart for his own good. Not when it came to Yorkies. He was under the mistaken impression they were squirrels and in desperate need of being chased.

Max lunged.

He pulled the leash from my hand.

"Watch out!" I cried.

The wind took my words and sent them in the opposite direction.

Max ran toward the old lady at full speed.

Her dog, seeing a behemoth bearing down upon them, yipped.

The old lady turned and saw Max. Or perhaps she saw me sprinting after him. Either way, her face contorted into an Edvard Munch painting. She screamed. She also let go of her little dog's leash.

The Yorkie did the only sensible thing. It ran.

"Max!" I screamed.

My dog ignored me.

Fortunately, he ran right past the old lady with her bent back and probably brittle hips. Max focused on the little dog who ran in circles, darting and weaving and yipping madly.

"Catch that awful beast." The older lady didn't sound brittle. She sounded mad as hell.

I ran past her. "Max!"

If he heard me, he gave no indication. He was too busy trying to land one of his paws on the yipping squirrel.

"Max!"

One of his paws came within a hair's breadth of pinning the dog to the ground.

"Get that hellhound away from my dog!" Her voice squeaked, especially on the last words. Apparently her pitch mimicked a dog whistle because both dogs turned and looked at her.

Then the Yorkie ran again. This time in a straight line. Toward the pond.

Max gave chase.

Oh dear Lord. "No!"

My words came too late—that or they weren't emphatic enough. The little dog sailed over the water, a silky brown bit of fluff caught in a gust of wind. Then he hit the surface.

Who knew such a little dog could make such a big splash?

"Elmer." The woman sounded distraught.

Max, who'd slid to a stop at the water's edge, looked disappointed.

I gripped my side where my ribs felt as if they were impaling my lungs

"He can't swim." The woman wrung her hands.

She was wrong. Elmer was swimming—dog paddling valiantly—toward the island.

I grabbed Max's leash. "Wrong way, Elmer!"

Elmer ignored me. Instead, he scrambled up the bank of the island, soaking wet and shivering with cold. Poor Elmer, he looked more like an alien than a dog.

"Bad dog." I shook my finger in Max's face.

Tell a Labrador he's done something naughty and his eyes and ears will droop. He might even hang his head. Max is not a Labrador. He didn't look remotely repentant.

"How are you going to get him off the island?" asked the woman.

Me?

"It's your dog's fault he's out there."

Be that as it may, Elmer was going to have to swim back.

"Elmer." The woman tottered toward the pond, leaned out over the water, and called again.

If she fell into the pond. I'd have to go in after her.

I reached for the back of her coat, ready to grab the fabric and haul her backward if her weight shifted forward.

Elmer sat down and looked at us. He showed no inclination to return to the water. Smart dog.

"Elmer!" Her voice quavered. She turned and glared at me. "It can't be good for him to be so cold. You've got to rescue him."

The pond wasn't big enough for boats. There was no way to get to the island without getting in the water. I'd been in that water. I wasn't getting in it again.

"Elmer's all I have and this—" the woman wiped her eyes "—is your fault."

She could play the guilt card all day long. No way, no how was I getting in that pond.

"Is there a problem, ladies?"

I turned.

The first thought that popped into my head was *Robbie Harney followed me here.*

The second was *why?*

The third was *who cares? Thank God he's here.*

"That beast—" the old lady pointed at Max who wagged his tail and offered up a doggy grin "—chased Elmer into the pond."

"Where is Elmer now?"

Elmer yipped.

There were so many things I wanted to say to Robbie Harney. None of them particularly nice. None of them particularly helpful since offending our only offer of aid seemed a bad plan.

He stood at the edge of the pond looking like Oliver Barrett in *Love Story* and rubbed his chin.

"I doubt Elmer will return to shore when the Weimaraner is waiting for him."

So Robbie did have a modicum of sense. I'd doubted that after he offered Stormy money to go away.

"Perhaps you and your dog should move away, Mrs. Russell." He pointed to a hilltop on the other side of the pond.

The old woman regarded me with beady brown eyes—eyes that were almost lost beneath drooping lids. "You know her?"

"I do," said Robbie.

"She dropped her dog's leash."

Robbie's mouth twisted as if he were trying not to smile. "It appears you dropped your dog's leash as well."

Now the woman's mouth twisted. She did not look as if she was fighting a smile. More a snarl. At me. And Max.

"My name is Ellison Russell, and I'm terribly sorry this happened." I extended my hand. "I'd be happy to pay for Elmer's next trip to the groomer's." I knew from experience that Elmer would not be smelling like roses when he came out of the water.

The old woman looked at my hand as if she might catch something if she touched it—even through her gloves. An awkward few seconds passed then she too extended a hand. "Bernice Billings. What if Elmer is hurt?"

I scowled down at Max. "I'll pay the vet bills too."

"He's traumatized."

I shifted my gaze from Max back to Bernice. Did she expect me to pay for a doggie shrink?

Out on the island, Elmer yipped.

"He sounds just fine to me. Again, I'm very sorry this happened. Now, I'll get out of the way so you and Mr. Harney can convince Elmer to come back." Max and I continued on the path around the pond. We reached the opposite side and ventured into the grass, climbing a gently sloping hill. The park had begun life as a golf course—all the hills sloped gently.

At the top, we stopped and turned.

Below us, Bernice and Robbie were still trying to entice Elmer back into the water.

The little dog no longer hid behind the tree. He sat on his tiny haunches at the pond's edge, showing not the slightest inclination to re-enter the cold water.

Bits of the woman's pleas reached me. "Elmer...treat...come."

Elmer did not look convinced.

Robbie's voice joined Bernice's. "Elmer..."

Elmer was having none of it. He lay down on the leaf-strewn ground and rested his head on his paws.

Bernice and Robbie gave up calling to the dog and talked to each other.

Whatever Robbie was saying, Bernice did not agree. She shook her head. She pointed to the hill where Max and I waited. She stomped her boot.

Robbie shook his head, pulled off his sweatshirt, and deposited it on a nearby bench. Next he kicked off his shoes and pulled of his socks. His sweatpants were next. He stood in the chill October air in nothing but shorts and a t-shirt.

He fiddled with his wrist and something gold flashed in the late afternoon light. A watch? He handed it to Bernice then approached the edge of the pond.

He wouldn't...

He couldn't...

He did.

Robbie Harney, a young man I'd never liked, jumped into the duck pond to rescue Elmer.

Elmer cocked his head at this new development.

Max did too.

It's possible my head was tilted as well.

After a brief swim, Robbie climbed onto the island and reached for Elmer.

The little dog, faced with a dripping stranger and the prospect of re-entering the cold water, bobbed and weaved like Muhammad Ali. Robbie crouched and held out his hand. He said something—the distance and the wind made it impossible to hear.

Elmer yipped.

Elmer did that a lot.

Robbie remained low to the ground, presumably telling Elmer sweet lies about how nice the water was.

Minutes passed.

On the opposite bank, Bernice clasped her hands in front of her heart.

Finally, Elmer ventured forward.

Robbie grabbed the little dog's leash. With the leash in hand, picking up Elmer was easy. Holding him looked like more of a problem. The dog wriggled and squirmed.

Robbie wrapped the leash around his hand and eased into the water.

A moment later, Elmer was in his owner's arms and Robbie was pulling on his sweatshirt and sweatpants over his wet clothes.

Bernice returned his watch and he fastened it on his wrist then patted Elmer on the head.

Even from my distant perch on the hill, I could see that Bernice was looking at Robbie as if he was Steve Austin at the end of a *Six Million Dollar Man* episode—as if he was a hero.

The hero sat down on the park bench and pulled on his socks and shoes.

When he was fully dressed, he stood.

Both he and Bernice looked up at me.

I tightened my hold on Max's leash and waved.

Robbie waved back. Bernice did not. She unbuttoned the top buttons of her coat, pressed Elmer against her chest, and shuffled off.

Robbie walked toward me.

I descended the hill to meet him. "Thank you."

"It was no problem."

"We both know that's not true."

He grinned and for an instant, I understood why Grace found him so appealing. Then I remembered Brooks, cold as marble on a table in the morgue, and shivered.

Robbie pushed up the sleeves to his sweatshirt and the gold watch flashed on his wrist. A Rolex. Henry had owned one just like it. It was an expensive watch for a young man. A very expensive watch.

First ten thousand dollars for Stormy. Now the watch.

He followed my gaze to his wrist. “It belonged to my grandfather.”

“It’s a nice watch.”

“It is,” he agreed. “A family heirloom. I should go. It’s cold out here.”

The clothes next to his skin were wet. He had to be freezing. “Thank you, again.”

“You’re welcome.” He turned and jogged away.

Max and I watched him go. Perhaps I’d been wrong about Robbie Harney. Perhaps he was a nice young man. Perhaps not. I knew a little something about Rolex watches. My late husband collected them and the one on Brooks’ wrist was a newer model. Why had he lied?

Max and I jogged home to the beat of *bad dog, bad dog, bad dog*.

Max, being Max, wasn’t particularly concerned with my ire. He knew I’d forgive him...eventually.

We entered the kitchen, which smelled of Aggie’s chili. My mouth watered. Max flopped on the floor and fixed his gaze on the pot bubbling on the stove.

“I’m glad you’re home,” said Aggie. “Olivia Forde called. She says if you want the Chinese panels, you need to let her know right away.”

“Did she leave a number?”

Aggie shook her head and her earrings, grinning jack-o-lanterns in honor of the holiday, bobbed. They matched her black muumuu. Someone had gone so far as to embroider spider webs on the fabric. “No. No number.”

“Her card is in the study.” I paused at the kitchen door and looked back. Aggie with her pumpkin colored hair was stirring the chili. Max was lolling. “You look very nice,” I said. “Very festive. Where’s Grace?” She’d lost no time going out as soon as her grounding was over.

"Out with Peggy and Debbie and Donna. She said she'd be home early."

I nodded then hurried down the front hall to the study. Olivia's business card still lay in the center of the blotter on Henry's desk. I picked up the phone and dialed.

Olivia answered on the third ring. "Hello."

"Olivia, this is Ellison Russell calling. I definitely want the panels."

"Fabulous," she cooed. "We'll decorate the room around them. They'll become family heirlooms."

Henry's study held all sorts of things he'd imagined would become family heirlooms. "Do you know someone who can appraise my husband's collection of Toby jugs?"

"The ones on the shelves behind the desk?"

The jugs with their ruddy faces and tricorne hats were staring at me now. Glaring as if they knew I intended to sell them to the highest bidder. "Exactly. They've never been my favorites."

"I'll find someone to look at them."

We hung up and I considered Henry's heirlooms. It was remarkably easy to let them go—to sell them. Probably as easy as it had been for the thief to sell PeeWa's beloved panels. What kind of thief took the things they'd stolen to another city? A smart one...

NINETEEN

I picked up the phone and put it down, glared at it for a moment, then picked it up again. I dialed the first three digits of Anarchy's number and returned the receiver to the cradle. It was too late to catch him at the office. Maybe he was at a Halloween party. One thing was certain, wherever he was, he wasn't wearing a pink suit. What kind of costume would he wear? Sherlock Holmes? The Waco Kid? Superman?

My suspicions were too amorphous to share. I wouldn't bother him. Not tonight.

Ding dong.

"I'll get it," Aggie called.

I met her in the foyer, pleased with a reason to abandon the telephone. Aggie held a bowl filled with enough candy to give half the children in the city—the city, not the neighborhood—cavities.

We opened to the door to a chorus. "Trick or treat."

Yes, the children wore coats over their costumes. Yes, they were still adorable.

Raggedy Ann was the first to hold up her plastic pumpkin.

Aggie dropped three pieces of candy into the pumpkin's depths. Later, in an hour or so, the children at the door would be older. The older kids eschewed pumpkins in favor of pillowcases. For now, a herd of pumpkins jostled forth, eagerly awaiting their candy.

Aggie filled them. Three pieces each.

A second chorus, this time, "Thank you!" The goblins and princesses and ghosts ran off to the next house. Well, not the *next* house. That house belonged to Margaret Hamilton. It was dark as sin and the children knew better than to disturb a real witch on Halloween. They ran through her yard.

Hopefully she didn't notice. If she did, they'd all wake up with warts on their noses or their candy transformed to laxatives.

Aggie closed the door. "This is my favorite holiday. No presents to buy. No fancy meals to prepare. Just fun and candy."

Ding dong.

A second crew held out their pumpkins and cried, "Trick or treat."

Aggie repeated the process. Three pieces in each pumpkin.

She closed the door and I asked, "Just how much candy did you buy?"

"Enough."

"Enough to send every kid in the neighborhood into a sugar coma?"

"Some of the kids who come here won't be from this neighborhood."

That was true. Parents from neighborhoods where trick or treating wasn't safe drove their children to my neighborhood. "Give them four."

Aggie grinned. "The chili is ready if you'd like to eat."

"Where's Max?"

Aggie paled.

Under normal circumstances, the dog would be greeting children and angling for candy. That he was missing at the same time an unattended pot of meat and beans simmered on the stove did not bode well.

Ding dong.

"You take care of the kids. I'll check on the chili."

In the kitchen, Max was still flopped on the floor. Snoring. Apparently chasing Yorkies into ponds was grueling work.

I moved the chili pot to the back burner, well out of the reach of his meat hook paws. On the other front burner sat the cast iron skillet Aggie used to brown meat. She was particular about that skillet, rinsing it with warm water, wiping it with a clean cloth, then drying it on the stove on low heat. I turned off the burner and let the pan sit.

The scent of chili hung in the air and my stomach rumbled. I opened the cabinet, took out a bowl, and ladled in a healthy serving.

Ding dong.

Aggie had lots of customers. Well, she had more than enough candy to handle them. Aggie's chili called for cheese and chopped onions. I put the bowl down on the counter and opened the fridge.

Ding dong.

That was strange.

Ding dong.

"Aggie?" I called.

There was no answer.

I pushed open the door from the kitchen to the front hall. "Aggie? Are you all right?"

Silence was the only answer.

I hurried down the hallway. "Aggie?"

Ding dong.

My housekeeper lay on the floor. Candy surrounded her. Snickers and Milky Ways and Paydays. Funny what you notice when time slows down...

I raced to her. "Aggie!"

She didn't move.

Blood run down her cheek. I searched for a pulse, found one, and released a ragged breath. "Aggie, what happened?" I asked.

A creepy-crawly-not-alone sensation trickled down my neck and froze my spine.

I didn't turn. Didn't dare. Instead I glanced at the mirror that hung above the bombe chest.

My heart leapt from my chest to my throat. From there it ricocheted about, finally landing in the pit of my stomach.

A clown—THE clown—stood behind me and he held a gun.

"Aggie?" My voice shook.

The clown was sneaking up on me like a character in a scary Abbot and Costello movie.

Ding dong.

The clown shifted his gaze to the door.

I struggled to my feet and ran. Down the hallway. Toward the kitchen. Toward the back door.

I didn't make it. He grabbed the back of my shirt, nearly choking me. The cold muzzle of a gun touched my neck. I was going to die. Killed by a clown.

Crash!

The sound came from the kitchen.

"Who's here?" he demanded.

"No one," I squeaked.

"Yeah, right."

He shoved me through the door.

Max looked up from the broken bowl and mess of chili on the floor and growled.

"Shut the dog up. I don't want to hurt him."

Well, there was a blessing. He didn't want to hurt Max. Me, he'd kill, but the dog would carry on.

"Max," I said. "It's all right."

It wasn't and Max knew it.

"Please, let me go to him."

The clown shoved me again. I lunged forward, slipped on a chili bean, and careened into the stove.

The dog scooted out of my way and growled again.

"Max." I lay my hand on his head. "Hush." Then I turned and looked at the clown.

He held a gun—something cheap and disposable, a Saturday night special. That I found the costume more terrifying than the gun didn't speak well of my metal prowess, but the clown's skin was white, his nose was red, his eyes black as tar. And his mouth—it was stretched in an obscene grin.

"You don't have to do this." My voice shook. "I have a daughter. She's already lost her father."

"Shut up."

I shut up. Briefly. If I was going to die, there were things I wanted to know first. "Why?"

"You had to go poking around."

"I didn't poke."

"Stormy Harney?" He spat the name.

Maybe I'd poked a little bit.

"I know you had Tafft call me about the things missing from PeeWa Asbury's place."

Not guilty. I hadn't known who Hunter called.

"He said you discovered the theft."

I had done that. "Detective Jones knows everything I know." He didn't. I hadn't called. I ignored the itch on the tip of my nose and put one hand behind my back.

The clown shook his head. "If you'd told him, I'd already be in jail."

Max growled again.

"Shush." My free hand closed around his collar. He pulled against my hold for a few seconds then relented, whining his displeasure.

"Why kill Brooks?" I asked.

"Brooks shortened the timeline. Who would have thought a heroin addict would make it to twenty-five?" He shook his head and the light reflected off the red ball of his nose.

Shortened the timeline?

Ding dong.

"Popular house for trick or treating." He might have been making conversation at a cocktail party. Except, he was a *clown*. A terrifying clown with a gun.

I nodded. "There are lots of people around." Would he hear what I wasn't saying? That someone would hear the shot. That help would arrive. That he would be caught.

Of course, I'd be bleeding out on top of a broken porcelain bowl and the chili Max hadn't managed to snarf down. My fingers closed around the handle of Aggie's cast iron skillet.

"What timeline?"

"I was going to put the money back. I had a plan, all I needed was a couple more months. I figured Brooks would never see twenty-five."

"But Brooks didn't die."

He shook his head. The painted grin on his face was truly horrifying. "Not only did he not die. He started asking questions."

"Charles Dix and John Phillips."

"Together they would have figured out there were funds missing from the trust. Brooks scheduled meetings with both of them. They could have put the pieces together."

"And Hunter Tafft?"

"Brooks was going to have him request an audit. I couldn't let that happen."

"So you killed him." Poor Brooks. Murdered because his birthday was looming and he'd asked questions about his money.

"He was a waste anyway."

"He was turning his life around."

"Working at a haunted house? Yeah, right. I did the Harneys a favor."

A sound penetrated the backdoor and we both turned our heads.

"What was that?" he demanded.

"No idea." *Please let it not be Grace. Please let it not be Grace. Please let it not be Grace.* I tightened my grip on the skillet. "You stole PeeWa's panels." My voice rose on the word panels so it sounded as if I was asking a question. I wasn't.

He scratched his painted on eyebrow. "I had to get the money somewhere."

I stared at him. The man beneath the makeup might actually be scarier than the clown. He had no conscience. No remorse.

"You stole from other clients."

He shrugged. "They won't miss it."

Ding dong.

He pulled a stool away from the counter and sat. "Like I said, popular house. Looks like we might need to wait a while." He looked around my kitchen. "Do you have anything to drink?"

He wanted a drink? "There's wine in the refrigerator."

"Any scotch?"

I shook my head. "No." My nose itched like hell. There was an ocean of scotch in the living room. Everything from single malts like Bladnoch to blends like Johnnie Walker. What the living room didn't have was a skillet, and I was loathe to let go of my only weapon.

"Just wine. I'll get it." I tried to sound eager, as if there was something I wanted in the refrigerator.

"Don't—" he thrust the gun in my direction "—move." He stood, crossed to the fridge and opened the door.

Dammit. He was too far away. If I rushed at him with the skillet and he turned, I'd be as good as dead.

He pulled a bottle of Blue Nun from the bottle rack. "How long has this been open?"

"Since yesterday."

He pulled the cork from the bottle. "Where do you keep your glasses?"

I jerked my chin toward the cabinet.

He took one down and filled it to the rim.

Great. The only thing worse than an evil clown with a gun was a drunk evil clown with a gun.

Ding dong.

He resumed his seat. "Those kids just keep coming. Lucky for you."

Funny. I didn't feel very lucky. A moment passed then I asked. "What did you do with the money?"

"Lost it in the market." He took a long sip of wine. "I'm going to put it back. The Harneys will never know."

Ding dong.

Ding dong.

Ding dong.

"Someone wants some candy," he observed.

I said nothing. I was too busy looking at the back door. Had the shadow I spotted belonged to a person? *Please let it not be Grace.* I made myself look at the painting on the other side of the room.

Ding dong.

He shifted his gaze to the door to the front hall. "Those kids, they don't give up. Too bad you can't reward their perseverance."

I shifted my gaze to the back door. The handle turned.

I looked away, terrified I'd bring attention to whoever was entering. *Please let it not be Grace.*

Ding dong.

The door flew open and my father leapt into the kitchen. He was armed with a tire iron, which, in the general scheme of things, was about as useful as a cast iron skillet against a gun.

Max barked. I lost my hold on his collar.

The dog launched himself into the air, teeth bared and a ridge of hair the size of the Rockies standing up on his back.

The clown pulled the trigger. *Bang!* A bullet whizzed by my head. Then the clown turned and took aim at my father.

Bang!

I lifted the heavy skillet off the stove, extended my arms as if I was reaching for a backhand ace, and swung.

Thunk!

There was a sickening sensation of breaking bone. There was blood. So much blood. And there was an unconscious clown on the kitchen floor.

"Are you all right?" I demanded.

My father held his arm and blood welled through his fingers. "Fine. You?"

"He missed."

Max stood over the clown, looking ready to rip him limb from limb if he moved a single muscle.

I kicked the gun into the far corner of the kitchen, snatched the receiver from the cradle and called for help. "We need the police and an ambulance! Two ambulances." One for Aggie and my father.

The other for the clown. Aggie! I needed to check on Aggie. I gave the operator my name and address and hung up the phone.

My father looked down at the prone clown. "He would have shot me dead."

"Yes." There was no point sugarcoating it.

"You saved me." Daddy sounded bewildered. "I came here to save you."

I walked toward the door to the hall—shuffled really, I'd never felt so exhausted. "Let's just say we saved each other and call it a day."

Ding dong.

"Who *is* that?"

I didn't expect an answer but my father grinned and said, "Grace."

That stopped me in shuffling tracks. "Grace?" My daughter had been ringing the bell over and over and over again?

"She was at Peggy's house and decided she wanted to come home. I gave her a ride. She looked through the backdoor window, saw the clown with the gun, and flagged me down before I pulled out of the driveway." Of course she had. Daddy would never pull away until she was safely in the house. "She's been ringing the bell to distract the clown."

I closed my eyes on the red haze that took over my vision. Sweet nine-pound baby Jesus, why had they put themselves at risk? What would she have done if the clown answered the door? "Why not call the police?"

"We didn't think there was time, and both your neighbors have their lights out, so we didn't have a phone."

I raised my brows and lowered my chin.

"Grace was in no danger." If that was true, why did he sound defensive?

"Do you know what you'd say to me if I rushed into a room where a man was holding you at gunpoint?"

"Thank you?"

"Ha."

"You saved me, Ellison. If you hadn't hit him with that skillet, I'd be dead. Thank you." He meant it. He understood, even if it that understanding was fleeting, that I possessed some strength. That I was more than just his little girl.

My throat swelled. "You're welcome."

The door from the hallway swung open, revealing my housekeeper and daughter. Aggie was nearly as pale as the clown and she leaned on Grace. Heavily. At least she was up, walking, breathing. A weight lifted from my chest.

She stared at the clown on the floor. "I'm so sorry." Her voice was faint. "I let him in."

"Don't be ridiculous," I said. "This is not your fault." The adrenalin that had flooded my system had ebbed completely and my legs wobbled. I rested my hip against the counter.

"Who is he?" asked Grace

I stared down at the clown who looked less scary but more horrifying with blood seeping from his head. "It's Jay Fitzhugh."

The police arrived. And the paramedics. And the neighbors, a bunch of ghouls gathered at the bottom of the driveway—it *was* Halloween.

Despite my protests that Aggie and Daddy deserved immediate care, the emergency personnel insisted on loading Jay into an ambulance first—some foolishness about traumatic head injury. Maybe I'd care about Jay's head tomorrow. Tonight I didn't have much sympathy.

Of course, someone called Mother. She blew into my kitchen with all the power of a tornado.

"What. Happened?" She glared at me. Whatever had happened, it had to be my fault.

"A man broke into our house," said Grace.

"Why?" she demanded.

To kill me didn't seem like an answer that would soothe Mother's nerves. Unfortunately, no other reason came to mind.

"We're all fine." Grace offered up a conciliatory smile.

"You are not. Your grandfather has been shot. He's outside with a paramedic now."

"Grazed," I muttered. The paramedics had assured me neither my father nor Aggie were seriously hurt.

"Do not trivialize this, Ellison."

"I'm not."

Cold, hard annoyance settled onto Mother's face. "You could have been killed."

She wasn't wrong. I sympathized with her. I wasn't exactly pleased that my daughter had decided to take so much initiative.

"Ellison!"

My head swiveled. I should have known Anarchy would turn up. He always did.

"What. Happened?" He sounded like Mother.

Explaining everything in front of Mother was a remarkably poor idea. "It's a long story."

Two sets of arms crossed. Ugh.

"Can we sit down in the living room? Please?"

"Fine." Mother took my arm and marched me down the hallway, directly to the most comfortable chair in the house. I sank into it.

"Do you want a drink?" she asked.

"Scotch."

She splashed some amber liquid into an old-fashioned, paused, then poured a tot into a second glass. "Detective Jones, would you like a drink?"

He looked as if he wanted to say *yes*. "No, thank you. I'm on duty."

Mother sniffed. Then she brought me my drink.

I wrapped my fingers around the glass and took a small sip. The scotch burned the back of my throat and warmed my stomach.

Mother perched on the edge of the couch. "Now, tell me what happened."

"He killed Brooks Harney."

Mother paled and worked her jaw. She looked mad enough to spit nails. "What was he doing here?"

"Shouldn't you be with Daddy?" I asked.

She glanced at the door, clearly torn. On the one hand, she should be with her husband. On the other, reading me the riot act would be deeply satisfying.

"Daddy *was* shot."

"Grazed," she replied.

My own words used against me.

"Grace is with him," she added.

I recognized defeat when I saw it. I took another sip and began. "Aggie answered the door, he cold-cocked her with his gun and came inside."

"And held you at gunpoint?"

"Yes."

"Why?" Mother demanded.

I glanced at Anarchy. Couldn't he interject? He sat stiff in an easy chair, apparently content to let Mother ask the questions.

"He thought I knew what he'd been up to."

"Did you?" Why, when Anarchy did ask a question, was it the one I didn't particularly want to answer?

"I suspected."

"And you didn't tell me?" The "cop" expression was evident in his brown eyes. Cold. Hard. All business.

"She's always been secretive," said Mother.

"I have not!" Had I? "I didn't think you'd believe me."

"I believed you when you reported a murder and there was no body."

There was that. And *that* was hard to argue.

Mother put her scotch down on the coffee table. She straightened her spine and crossed her ankles. She donned a *grande dame* expression—a combination of look-down-her-nose, curl-the-corner-of her-lower-lip, and head tilt—that perfectly communicated her disappointment with me. "When are you going to stop finding bodies? It's very disruptive."

Disruptive? "I don't go looking for them, Mother." Tired as I was, my back stiffened. If she wanted an argument, I'd give her one.

"Yes, well, perhaps you should try looking the other way."

"Back to Fitzhugh."

Anarchy's comment distracted me. My witty rejoinder flitted away, leaving me with nothing to say.

Mother was never at a loss for words. "Horrible man."

Anarchy shifted in his chair. "I think you should come down to the station."

"Tonight?" I squeaked.

"Absolutely not. Just look at her. She's exhausted."

Did I look exhausted or did Mother not want me out in public in my running clothes? It didn't matter. I wasn't going anywhere. "Tonight, I need to rest. I'll tell you everything tomorrow."

TWENTY

Grace had questions, so I let her skip school. Telling my daughter what had led to a demented clown taking over our kitchen seemed more important than Algebra II. It also seemed more important than driving to the police station.

If it had been an hour later, I would have put her off until after we visited Aggie in the hospital. But it was early and hopefully Aggie was still asleep.

I poured myself a cup of coffee. "Shoot."

Maybe not the best thing to say with two bullet holes in our kitchen walls. I needed to keep a handyman on retainer.

"Do you want to put on some lipstick?"

That was her question? "Why?"

"You look wan."

Wan? "And..."

She squirmed on her stool. "Detective Jones is coming over."

"Why?"

"I talked to him last night after you went upstairs. He said he'd come here and save you a trip to the station."

"Did he now?"

"I should have waited until your second cup to tell you."

Hmph. "No, on the lipstick."

"Suit yourself."

I intended to. "When we're done, we need to go see Aggie." I took another sip of perfect coffee. "And your grandfather."

She nodded. "So what happened?"

"I'm not a hundred percent sure on all of this."

She shrugged. "Just tell me."

"Jay Fitzhugh embezzled funds from the Harneys' Trust and invested the money in the stock market." I paused. "At least that's what he said." It could be he'd invested the money in expensive coats for pretty young women. "He expected Brooks would overdose and die. If that happened, Jay had several years before the trust needed to disperse funds."

"But Brooks didn't die."

"Brooks didn't die, and going to jail for embezzlement didn't appeal to Jay."

Tap, tap, tap.

I peered through the glass in the backdoor and my mouth went dry. Since when had Anarchy become a backdoor friend?

Grace leapt off her perch on the edge of the counter and let him in. "Mom was just telling me about Mr. Fitzhugh."

I wet my mouth with a large gulp of coffee. "How is he?"

"He's got a concussion but he'll recover."

"Good." On so many levels. First off, he'd have to pay for what he'd done. Second, I hadn't killed him. "Coffee?"

"I'll help myself."

Anarchy was getting entirely too comfortable in my kitchen. He opened a cabinet, selected a mug, and poured.

"He confessed. To everything. Killing Brooks. Killing Charles Dix. The attempt on John Phillips."

"Wait," said Grace. "He killed Charles Dix?"

Anarchy nodded. "When Brooks came back to Kansas City, he asked for an accounting of the trust. Dix pulled the paperwork and noticed something was off. Apparently he confronted Fitzhugh after Harney's murder so Fitzhugh killed him."

"And the antiques?" I asked.

"He's been systematically stealing from trusts he manages and selling through out of town dealers."

"I thought as much."

"What happens now?" asked Grace.

"He'll be charged with the murders and aggravated assault if

Aggie or your grandfather wish to press charges. The bank will be pursuing grand larceny charges."

Grace swished the remains of her juice in the bottom of her glass. "So he's going to jail."

"For a long time." Anarchy rubbed his chin. "You know you should have called the police last night."

"I didn't think we had time." Grace's voice took on the defensive tone that is unique to teenagers—half apologetic, half defiant.

"If anyone scolds Grace it will be me."

Anarchy looked at me expectantly. He was waiting for me to tell Grace to be safe, to be careful. "Everyone makes choices. Everyone balances risks. What I hope for you, honey, is that you weigh the risks and rewards before you take action. I don't want you to live your life packed in cotton, but I don't want you to be reckless either."

A few seconds passed. Then a few more.

Finally, Grace came over to me, wrapped her arms around my neck, and rested her head on my shoulder. "Thanks, Mom."

No one sets out to limit their children. It happens by accident. And sometimes, by accident, parents do something right.

JULIE MULHERN

Julie Mulhern is the *USA Today* bestselling author of The Country Club Murders. She is a Kansas City native who grew up on a steady diet of Agatha Christie. She spends her spare time whipping up gourmet meals for her family, working out at the gym and finding new ways to keep her house spotlessly clean—and she's got an active imagination. Truth is—she's an expert at calling for take-out, she grumbles about walking the dog and the dust bunnies under the bed have grown into dust lions.

The Country Club Murders
by Julie Mulhern

THE DEEP END (#1)

GUARANTEED TO BLEED (#2)

CLOUDS IN MY COFFEE (#3)

SEND IN THE CLOWNS (#4)

Henery Press Mystery Books

And finally, before you go...
Here are a few other mysteries
you might enjoy:

BOARD STIFF

Kendel Lynn

An Elliott Lisbon Mystery (#1)

As director of the Ballantyne Foundation on Sea Pine Island, SC, Elliott Lisbon scratches her detective itch by performing discreet inquiries for Foundation donors. Usually nothing more serious than retrieving a pilfered Pomeranian. Until Jane Hatting, Ballantyne board chair, is accused of murder. The Ballantyne's reputation tanks, Jane's headed to a jail cell, and Elliott's sexy ex is the new lieutenant in town.

Armed with moxie and her Mini Coop, Elliott uncovers a trail of blackmail schemes, gambling debts, illicit affairs, and investment scams. But the deeper she digs to clear Jane's name, the guiltier Jane looks. The closer she gets to the truth, the more treacherous her investigation becomes. With victims piling up faster than shells at a clambake, Elliott realizes she's next on the killer's list.

PRACTICAL SINS
FOR COLD CLIMATES

Shelley Costa

A Val Cameron Mystery (#1)

When Val Cameron, a Senior Editor with a New York publishing company, is sent to the Canadian Northwoods to sign a reclusive bestselling author to a contract, she soon discovers she is definitely out of her element. Val is convinced she can persuade the author of that blockbuster, The Nebula Covenant, to sign with her, but first she has to find him.

Aided by a float plane pilot whose wife was murdered two years ago in a case gone cold, Val's hunt for the recluse takes on new meaning: can she clear him of suspicion in that murder before she links her own professional fortunes to the publication of his new book?

When she finds herself thrown into a wilderness lake community where livelihoods collide, Val wonders whether the prospect of running into a bear might be the least of her problems.

Available at booksellers nationwide and online

Visit www.henerypress.com for details